LIGHTBULB MOMENTS
THROUGH THE EYES OF MEN

Stories of HOPE Vol 3
The Wake Up Call I Needed

REVIEWS

"As with the men in this book, it was a lightbulb moment that saw me rise above my own battle with mental health. The stories in this book are real and raw. They are about the process of overcoming past pain and regret to invoke change for good and testament to the fact that by holding onto hope you will find better days ahead."

Darius Boyd former NRL Representative – Speaker – Mental Health Advocate

"It is still rare to find a book such as this one that deals with the emotions of men. For all the talk about the way masculinity is having to adapt to 21st century society there is little media content reflecting the issue. Author Kerrie Atherton captures the dynamism of the often breathtaking "lightbulb moments" in the lives of fifteen men from very different backgrounds as they discover new meaning, fresh purpose and a true understanding of their own destiny."

Mike McCarthy former BBC Journalist – Founder 'Baton of Hope'.

"Once again Kerrie has managed to pull together a group of people to share their amazing stories of tragedy, wrong decisions, and their paths, but more importantly what they did to overcome their challenging times and come out the other side with purpose in life to help others. I know many of us can relate to "the wakeup call I needed" and I know this book will help so many people with their own struggles and journeys. I commend Kerrie on her time and efforts in publishing another amazing book."

Stuart Rawlins - Ex Detective - Mental Health Advocate - Stories of HOPE storyteller

DEDICATION

For all those searching for HOPE or
for a second chance,
this book is for you.

At the end of the day, when the lights go out,
we are all the same.

We are emotions in skin.

We are all

HUMAN

LIGHTBULB MOMENTS
THROUGH THE EYES OF MEN

Stories of HOPE Vol 3

The Wake Up Call I Needed

Compiled by Kerrie Atherton

Disclaimer:

This book is intended for adult readers only. It contains descriptions of mental health, drug use, assault, adult themes. Some readers may find this distressing. Reader discretion is advised.

This book is sold with the understanding that the authors are not offering any specific personal advice to the reader. For professional advice, seek the service of a suitable, qualified professional practitioner. The authors, compiler and publisher disclaim any responsibility for liability, loss or risk, personal or otherwise, that happens as a consequence of the use and application of any contents of this book.

The publisher is not responsible for any breach of confidence or confidentiality regarding names or places referred to throughout this book nor within each story.

Lightbulb Moments – Through The Eyes Of Men
Copyright ©2022 by Kerrie Atherton
https://storiesofhope.com.au
https://soulessenceinternational.com

Cover Art © 2022 https://russell-ink.com.au

ISBN SC: 978-0-6455992-0-6

NATIONAL
LIBRARY
OF AUSTRALIA

A catalogue record for this book
is available from the National Library of Australia

FOREWORD

A light-bulb moment is defined as a split second when we are struck by a sudden realisation, enlightenment, or inspiration.

It can come in many ways, and at many times in our lives. Perhaps we are lucky enough to experience them daily.

The life changing light-bulb moments in this book showcase the personal journeys of men of all ages at a time when male mental health has reached a crisis point around the world. Some of these flashes of awareness are observed in unexpected places: in the departure lounge of a Tokyo airport; in the middle of a terrorist attack in Paris; riding with a bikie gang on the New South Wales north coast and in the darkest depths of a high-security Australian prison.

This is the third book in the Stories of HOPE series. The worldwide platform was started five years ago by Kerrie Atherton, a counsellor, speaker and mental health advocate. Kerrie is a big-hearted person who has made it her mission to provide comfort and inspiration to a wider audience by sharing some of the incredible tales from speakers of her Stories of HOPE events who have climbed out of their hardest times.

Just like the people in this book, I too can relate to having overcome major hurdles just to keep afloat in life. Despite many self-doubts and insecurities arising from the trauma of my past, I was determined to pave the way for a better future, allowing me to achieve a dream far beyond what I could have ever imagined.

As I looked down the barrel of a television camera at CNN International in 1999, I experienced my own lightbulb moment. I was a pioneer Australian presenter, broadcasting live out of the US to more than 200 countries. Four years earlier, I was the first Aussie news reader on the relaunched BBC World News in London.

I had to pinch myself… is this really me, dressed to the hilt and wearing studio make-up in a high-profile position coveted by tens of thousands of other journalists?

As with many of the men in this book, early setbacks, self-doubts, and family trauma played havoc with my mental health. It shattered my confidence and left me doubting myself and my place in the world.

My father was a brilliant man — an advertising copywriter, radio/TV screenwriter and visual artist — who guided the early days of my career. Those days began when I was a fifteen-year-old schoolboy, writing unpaid sports stories at the weekend for a local newspaper on Sydney's lower north shore.

My Dad was my mentor who encouraged my early articles, helping me whip them into shape on a small, portable typewriter in his home office.

But he was also a recovering alcoholic and drug addict whose dramatic relapse after a decade of sobriety saw him take his own life at our family house five days before Christmas that same year. He left my mother with four school-age boys, the youngest turning five and preparing to start kindergarten. Suicide, a topic that is talked about on these pages, has a devastating effect on all those left behind.

The next setback happened 18 months later. Still reeling from my father's death, I was trying to finish school before looking for a job in journalism as I continued my part-time role as a weekend reporter.

My final year English teacher, who had taken an instant dislike to me, called my mother to the school for a special meeting. Knowing that my heart was set on a career in the media, the teacher informed my Mum that I would never make it in journalism so I should be steered into a different profession.

But despite my teacher's lack of belief in me, I landed a coveted cadetship at The Sydney Morning Herald later that year, beating hundreds of applicants to the position. I was just seventeen years old.

However, when I tried to move from newspapers to television several years later, I was faced with a third demoralising setback. At twenty-one, I struggled as I tried to make the transition to broadcast journalism as a rookie on-camera reporter. About four months into a new job at Channel 7 in Sydney, the chief of staff pulled me aside. He said to me: "You're never going to make it in television, I advise you to go back and work in newspapers again." The assistant news director, the bigger boss, who had given me the job in the first place, expressed a similarly negative sentiment when we met the next day: "You look too young on TV." he said. "It's just not working out."

This third setback may have crushed most people. But, by that stage in my life, I had become very determined in the wake of earlier disappointments. This time, another lightbulb moment caused me to realise that I had it inside me to prove these naysayers wrong. While it was clear that I was still weak as a TV reporter, I felt that all I needed was more time to learn the ropes and develop my skills.

Facing the sack, I was saved by the executive producer of Channel 7's nightly current affairs program. A veteran of media, he was impressed by my fearless interviewing technique and eye for a story when I'd sat down with him a few months earlier for a story for my old newspaper. He offered me a job within his team as a junior reporter. I gratefully accepted. A decade later, after overcoming more setbacks, I became the senior sports presenter for BBC World in London, sharing the studio set with famous broadcasters whom I'd admired on television for years.

Just like the remarkable man in one of the stories in this book, I was determined not to follow in my father's footsteps. His struggles with alcohol were always in my mind (my uncle and grandfather were also alcoholics) so I focused on staying fit and sharp to give me an edge when I was on the air. By this point, I had given up drinking completely.

Having achieved an unlikely dream in the UK, I then set the even loftier goal of making it as a TV anchor in the US. It took almost two years, but eventually, I cracked it. After working as reporter in local TV news for the NBC station in Denver, I was offered a job by CNN in early 1999, initially as a general news producer in its Atlanta newsroom. Anything is possible if you don't give up.

By the end of the year, I was given a full-time contract as an anchor. I had landed my dream job, presenting international sports on a much-watched, twice-daily show as part of a harmonious and supportive team. And, yes, my family, plus all the people back in Australia who told me I would never make it, were able to tune in.

LIGHTBULB MOMENTS – Through The Eyes Of Men, is a timely reminder that with enough hope and determination, you can turn your life around. From a young kid scrambling for my future, I managed to carve out a successful career as a television and radio broadcaster for more than a quarter of a century, while also working as an emcee, media trainer and digital journalist. It couldn't have happened had I not heeded the wake-up call within and faced up to my own doubts and insecurities. The CNN and BBC experience would open a magical chapter in Asia that saw me work as a broadcaster in exotic locations, from Manila to Mumbai, Singapore to Sri Petaling, Bangkok to Bangalore.

I returned to Australia in 2019 just before the pandemic. Since then, I have sat in the host's chair at Brisbane's 4BC as part of the Nine Radio network, while doing multi-platform reporting for ABC News. I have been a business and real estate TV presenter and stood in front of students as a guest tutor at three Australian universities. And volunteering every week for a community music radio station in Logan, south of Brisbane, is something that brings me a lot of laughter and joy.

Having read these inspirational Stories, I realise there are common threads between my own journey and those featured in the book. Dogged determination, resilience, persistence and finding our true voice have served us well. Simply being able to speak out and share is the beginning of healing pain, regret and disappointment.

Once we have found our chosen path, gratitude and giving back to life are essential for ensuring longevity. And whenever we have given up something that is not good for us — that could be drugs, alcohol, gambling or even low self-esteem — it is much easier when something positive replaces it.

While I am not advocating any dogma or belief — it is up to the individual to find out what works best for them — an antidote could come in the form of religion, spirituality, yoga, love of nature and giving back to life through charitable service. And, of course, having the courage to simply take that next step, even when everything seems lost.

Just keep moving forward and do your best.

So, as you read these Stories of HOPE, take a moment to reflect on your own light-bulb moments. Write them down if you want and connect the dots on your personal journey. Think about the miracles, however small, in your own life. This may even help you plan and develop your next steps.

And remember that a lightbulb moment may be all you need to know that anything is possible.

Jason Dasey

International TV and Radio Presenter

PREFACE

From a Lightbulb Moment, a Vision Grew

There is a venue on the Sunshine Coast, Queensland where lives have been transformed on the same night on the same week of every month. This is Stories of HOPE, which began with a simple idea linked with a big vision to spread the strongest message to anyone who is going through a challenge in life—the message that they are not alone and that there are others who have been on the same journey and have come out the other side with not only HOPE but a greater purpose than ever before.

It was 2017 when I Kerrie Atherton reached out to a small group of friends, daring to share my vision: to offer a brighter future to those who needed to hear a message of HOPE. I dreamed of reaching not only my local community on the Sunshine Coast but also the state of Queensland and branching out to all of Australia—maybe even the world. As I waited, sitting alone on a chair, the time I had set for this—my milestone event—was drawing near. But nobody had arrived. I began to entertain the thought that I might be left in the room with just my husband for company, and my dream might come crashing down before it had been given the chance to take flight. But then, as if in slow motion, people walked through the door one after the other. Thirty arrived, in total. This was it: my dream had just become a reality. This is where Stories of HOPE Australia began.

Over the past five years, a function room in the Sands Tavern in Maroochydore has become a place where people regularly come together for a common purpose—to find and to give HOPE. Many are broken, many have been through such devastating circumstances, many feel alone in their suffering, but this is a sacred place where they know they belong, with the knowledge that others have been where they are and understand what they are going through. People who know their pain and people who have stories of victory can testify to the fact that there is a light at the end of every tunnel and that HOPE is possible.

Stories of HOPE Australia has given a voice to the many who have taken to the stage to share their heart-wrenching and inspirational stories and it has provided a catalyst for transformation in those who attend to hear them. Everyone leaves the monthly event changed for the better, with a new sense of purpose and destiny they never dreamed to be possible. This is the power of Stories of HOPE Australia, and it had begun to spread across the globe with the release of the first book in the series, Stories of HOPE Australia: Everyday People, Extraordinary Stories in 2019, then followed by Volume two, Stories of HOPE Australia: Resilient People, Remarkable Stories in 2020.

In the weeks leading up to the launch of Volume two, Covid struck overseas, but had not yet reached our shores. The week after the launch the whole earth went into lockdown and our world as we knew it changed forever. As a result, the monthly events where we had gathered together over the past five years were closed down and everyone was confined to their homes. The only real way of connection was online. Being a connector and an empath along with seeing the immense amount of suffering and isolation going on around the globe my own mental health along with millions of others began to suffer.

Connection is vital for the human soul to flourish as is having a purpose and it seemed like I had lost mine. There is a famous verse, 'Without a vision people perish'. Uncertainty was closing in on everyone. Knowing that I had a choice to either sink or swim through this very hard time, I chose to look at what I could control, and I started to swim. I began interviewing people from all around the world online who had come out the other side of hard times and could be a role model of resilience to all. Hence the formation of Stories of HOPE Worldwide began.

During this time and in keeping with my new mantra of 'looking at what I could control' instead of allowing myself to be consumed with depression and apathy, I decided to upskill and enrolled in a Mental Health First Aid Course. I loved it so much I decided to become a Mental Health First Aid trainer. I wanted to learn as much as I could to enhance my skills as a counsellor and wellbeing coach to help the increasing number of people who were struggling with their mental health a number in fact that had reached an all-time high. Through this time, I also took part in a world first pilot training run by the 'Movember' organisation called, 'Men In Mind' for therapists who were counselling and supporting men going through mental health struggles. It became evident to me just how many men we were losing around the world to suicide with the rate of men here where I live on the Sunshine Coast in QLD at the time being 9% above the national average. Having supported so many men over the years through my work as a counsellor and also my involvement in the 12-step program, I decided to dedicate this book to the men of this world.

To all those who are struggling in silence, either through shame or fear, to all those who have stepped out and sought help, and for those yet to find their way. No matter what has happened in your life, you are not defined by your past. You don't have to wait for the 'wakeup call' or until life has fallen apart to change your destiny, Instead, I truly believe that by hearing and reading the lived experience stories of those who have gone through the hardest times and come out the other side, inspiration can be found by all. I hope you enjoy this the third book in my Stories of HOPE series LIGHTBULB MOMENTS – Through The Eyes Of Men and take comfort in the fact that, if hope can happen for the people in this book, it can happen for you also. This is the power of Stories of HOPE.

CONTENTS

ALEX GERRICK

A CEO'S BATTLE WITH PTSD
MELTDOWN IN TOKYO

"Every sinew of my brain became focused on the events at Narita Airport. After so many years lying to myself, I finally accepted that something was not right with my mind, and I reached out for help."

I will never forget my first day of school. Having been born in June created a particular dilemma for my parents: should I start school when I was four and a half, meaning that I would be much younger than my fellow classmates; or should I start a year later, when I was little more worldly? After many consultations with the school headmaster, they finally agreed on the second option. I was unhappy about it, but it gave me more time to play cowboys and Indians in my backyard and dream of new worlds to conquer.

That I was six months older than most of the other kids was not lost on me on that hot January morning the following year when I barged headfirst into the playground to officially start my schooling. Knowing that I could read and write better than most kids my age, I pranced around from new friend to new friend, with an arrogant swagger and confidence that would sometimes follow me into adulthood, much to the dismay of my detractors. As I marched onto the parade ground for my first ever school assembly, all I could think about was that this was the first day of the rest of my life.

Later that night, after dinner, I joined my father in the backyard, and together, we gazed at the trillions of stars that welcomed us to the emerging darkness. As we stared at the milky way, I asked my father the usually rhetorical question that most little kids ask on their first day of school, "What do you think I will be when I grow up, dad?" He momentarily inspected me with those fierce black eyes of his that usually frightened me when he was angry and replied with, "only your future has that answer, my son. But remember one thing, whatever you do, always look out for the little things in life first, for they will inevitably guide you to something bigger."

As I grew older, those words would drift in and out of my psyche. Perhaps it was because I would lose respect for my father over time, as I realised the extent of his secret life and how he sometimes treated my mother. Or maybe I was obsessed with my own arrogance that I failed to heed the mysteries of my past. In any case, as the disasters began to pile up with curious regularity, I was blinded to the little warning signs that could have helped me avert disaster.

However, if nothing more, I was a resilient bugger, who, by the time I reached 50, thought he had finally escaped a world of childhood trauma and several triggering events in his thirties to establish himself as a respected and much-admired leader in the federal public service. I was at the peak of my career as a senior bureaucrat with the Australian Public Service in Canberra and with the prospect of further advancement just around the corner. It may not have been what I expected when I gazed at the stars with my father all those years before, but I was proud of what I was able to achieve so far, especially given the secret I had been hiding for decades.

You see, I knew that I was suffering from a trauma-related disorder and associated mental illness, but I was too scared to do anything about it. I was afraid that as soon as I admitted that I had a problem, my whole world, and every relationship in it, would come crashing down on top of me. I was determined to hide my issues if it meant lying to everyone at work and to everyone who cared about me. As a result, almost overnight, I became the most outstanding actor in the world. I would get up in the morning, shower, put on my suit, and stride to work.

During the day, I would attend meetings, solve problems, help my staff and give speeches as if nothing was wrong. Then I would go home, have dinner, watch TV, and in the wee hours of the morning, my mind would begin to wander into forbidden places that no person should ever visit. I would catastrophize over stupid things, have inane conversations with myself, and sometimes even experience hallucinations that were downright scary. I would then have three or four hours of disturbed sleep, wake up and start the process all over again. It was a horrible way to live, exacerbated by the fact that I refused to discuss these issues with anyone who could possibly help me.

Something had to give eventually, and it began in the most sordid of ways. In mid-2014, a rumour started that I was having an affair with one of my staff members. Something in my psyche snapped. Soon after I descended into a totally dark place where my paranoia, that had laid dormant for so many years, started to take control of my senses.

By the beginning of 2015, I was looking for conspiracies everywhere. Apart from those in my team, and a few close friends at the senior levels, I trusted no-one in the organization.

As far as I was concerned, everyone was out to get me; everyone was talking about me. Deep down, I knew it was all irrational nonsense, but to think otherwise would have meant admitting that I had a problem, and there was no way I was ever going to do that. While I was content to allow my mental health to deteriorate, everything else in my life became a huge lie.

I was very fortunate that I had a brilliant team who supported me. The main pleasure I got from life during those terrible months was seeing them grow into something special. I had put a lot of effort into mentoring staff, and I could see it paying dividends. I knew that some people felt that I was too close to my staff but growing together with my team was the only thing that kept me sane at a time when my mental health was threatening to consume me.

Towards the end of 2015, things began to totally wear me down. I needed a holiday and in late September 2015 I decided to visit Europe for two weeks before meeting up with my wife, Miriam, for a week in Hong Kong. I was desperately hoping that this trip would be the antidote I needed to get me through the rest of the year unscathed.

In arranging my trip, I decided to stop off for a few nights in Tokyo, before flying to London. Tokyo was one of my favourite cities in the world and I was both enamoured and fascinated with Japan's unique culture and its people. When I landed at Narita airport, eight hours after departing from Brisbane, I felt a huge weight lift off my shoulders. It was if the burden of the previous twelve months or so at work was finally dissolved and I could sit back and enjoy myself for once.

I had a terrific time for those first few days: doing the obligatory tourist things such as visiting Tokyo Tower, exploring the wonderful Ueno Park and paying homage to Senso-Ji. On top of that, I gorged myself on the delicious local food, swallowed one or two glasses of chest-burning Saki and chatted with some amazing Japanese people. On my last day in Tokyo, a glorious sun-drenched Sunday, I took a bus tour to Mount Fuji, where at my third attempt in ten years, I finally got to see the famous summit from a cable car. It was the perfect way to end three fantastic days in this equally fantastic city.

That night, I was blessed with a rare trouble-free sleep and woke up early next morning to catch my shuttle bus to Narita airport. After I checked in and navigated my way through immigration and customs, I made my way to the airport lounge to have my last cup of coffee before boarding my British Airways flight to London Heathrow. As I shuffled along at a gentle pace, I pulled out my personal Nokia phone from my coat pocket to check if I had any messages from Australia. Although I kept my work iPhone safely stashed away in my office, my staff were given this number to call me in an emergency. Although I was grateful that there were no messages, I did notice that the battery was nearly flat and casually reprimanded myself for not charging it last night before I went to bed. Unperturbed, I walked into to the lounge, grabbed myself a coffee and searched for an electrical outlet. When I found a spare one, I dropped into the adjoining seat and opened my carry bag to pull out my charger.

Sometimes in life, you have that unerring feeling that something isn't right. As soon as I opened the bag's zipper, I obtained this sinking feeling inside my stomach that I forgot to unplug my phone charger from the socket in the bathroom when I packed my suitcase that morning. Suddenly nervous hands barged into the bag, pushing aside my passport, painkillers, novel and iPod. When I couldn't locate anything that remotely felt like a charger, I turned over my bag in panic and allowed gravity to drop out all its contents onto the ground.

For several minutes, I did nothing more than stare blindly at the assortment of goods scattered before me. I could feel the pangs of anger that always accompanied me when something didn't go to plan in my life gather intensity inside my lungs.

Back in 2000, I had met an incredible African American nurse named Delilah while visiting New York who taught me how to control my temper when things in my world seemed bleak. Desperate for help, I tried to connect with her accusing eyes to calm me down, but all I saw was the world collapsing around me.

Sure, it was only a mobile charger. When I landed in London, there would be plenty of time for me to locate a replacement. But common sense doesn't always placate people who are suffering from mental illness or a trauma-related disorder. And for me, this ridiculous little situation, as unimportant as it was, suddenly escalated into an earth-shattering event. Without thinking what I was doing, I quickly grabbed my carry bag and began to bang it onto the ground hoping that at any moment, the charger would miraculously appear before my eyes. But when it didn't emerge after all that hollering and thumping, I callously tossed the bag into the air, without any regard to anyone else in the lounge. Sure enough, it almost hit a burly Mediterranean man in the face, and the way he looked at me with his pitchfork eyes, suggested he wasn't going to accept an apology too readily. Predictably, we were soon shouting at each other, waving our arms about with violent intent. A lounge representative – a massive unit himself – put his large frame between us before the situation could escalate any further. He soon made some inquiries to some witnesses, and to my horror, asked me to leave the lounge.

Of course, given my agitated state of mind, this was just red rag to a bull. I screamed and shouted at him and called him every name under the sun, each of those insults proceeded with that uncouth F word. I was too stupid to realise it yet, but an international incident was fast becoming an unnerving reality. Imagine, a senior Australian bureaucrat arrested for public affray in an international airport! I was eventually saved from my own stupidity by a kindly Australian woman, who had also witnessed the fracas and promised the lounge rep that she would escort me outside. It wasn't the first time in my life that I had been rescued by a woman who had a better understanding of myself than I did.

A few hours later, safely on board my BA flight, I tried to pretend that what had happened at the lounge was nothing more than an isolated incident of madness. But as I immersed myself into the in-flight entertainment, I knew deep down that my behaviour had not been normal and that it was a symptom of a wider malaise that had been infecting me for some time. I spent the next few days wandering aimlessly around London. I had no plan, and my holiday was seemingly heading for disaster. I went to a football match at Wembley stadium and to this day, I still can't tell you anything about the game I watched other than England was playing Switzerland. My head was flooded by rain clouds, and I had no idea who I was anymore.

A few days later, I took the Eurostar to Paris and settled into a nice little hotel close to the Louvre. I was scheduled to do a short course on the French Revolution at the Sorbonne, and I looked forward to engaging my mind on something else other than my mental health. But as I was walking home one night after visiting the Eiffel Tower, I was suddenly hit by a golden flash of light.

Yes! It was the proverbial light bulb moment that we all crave for when we are on the edge of a precipice! As I was consumed by the unfolding beauty of a Paris twilight, every sinew of my brain became focused on the events at Narita Airport. After so many years lying to myself, I finally accepted that something was not right with my mind. No normal person would act that way about a misplaced phone charger. And man, wasn't it a scary realisation?

What happened after that moment of intense clarity remains an inconclusive blur. No, I am not finding excuses for my apathy, but not every light bulb moment has a happy ending or indeed, guarantees success. You see, although I had been given a warning shot across my bow, circumstances intervened which sent me spiralling down another path.

Over the next few days, I would pick up a debilitating stomach illness that left me gasping for air by the time I reached Hong Kong to meet my wife. All I could think about was dulling the intense pain that was ripping my intestines apart. By the time I got back to Australia, returned to work and then re-immersed myself into a very large workload, the shattered fragments of that lightbulb that went off in Paris were flickering aimlessly in the wind. I had lost my opportunity to take some positive action and redeem myself and it would cost me deeply.

Over the next few months, as we entered 2016, my mental health significantly declined. I was overcome with paranoia, anxiety, depression, and a restlessness that I hope will never experience again in my life. I knew something bad was about to happen, but I had no control over how these events were to play out. I was like a man rowing a boat full of holes in the open seas; hellbent on bailing out the water, while the holes were growing wider and wider apart. In effect, I was watching over my own demise.

My day of reckoning finally came in early 2016, when I became consumed by an issue at work. Due to its serious nature, I was convinced that my career, and everything that I had worked so hard for, would soon be over. This realisation led to a fit of vile depression that almost ended in suicide. If not for the intervention of a courageous work colleague, you might be reading a totally different story. After the issue was finally resolved in my favour, I commenced a yearlong counselling program with my therapist. One of the first things he forced me to do was admit that I had a problem. This time I was not going to let myself down. As I sat in my therapist's office, my father's words came back to haunt me.

'But remember one thing. Whatever you do, always look out for the little things in life first, for they will inevitably guide you to something bigger.'

Yes, dad, you were right. Leaving that charger behind in my hotel room was seemingly a little thing, but in reality, it was the key to unlocking something bigger – the state of my mental health and the traumas from my past that had been impacting me for years. However, I was too preoccupied with my own vanity to realise the importance of that light bulb moment and as a consequence, I almost paid with my life.

In March 2018 I left the Australian Public Service. I wanted to use the rest of my working life dedicated to helping people, especially middle-aged professional men, come to terms with trauma-related disorders and mental illness. I became CEO of the not-for-profit organization FearLess, and wrote a book based on personal experiences called A Season of Clouds. Through my work, I continue to encourage people not to discount the little warning signs that may one day save your life. Fortunately, our body and our mind frequently tell us that we are not on the right track. But we are resilient creatures, who can find the smallest strand of light inside the darkest tunnel. So, when that light bulb comes searching for you, don't ignore it like I did. Follow it, believe in it and you might surprise yourself in finding a permanent way out of the darkness.

ALEX GERRICK - CEO FEARLESS PTSD Organization – Deputy Chair ATL – Author of A Season of Clouds

Email: alex.gerrick@fearless.org.au

ANTON GUINEA

LEADING UNDER PRESSURE
FROM BURNS SURVIVOR TO LEADERSHIP COACH

"My whole world shifted, particularly after the explosion on the site in May 2021. It was like the missing piece that was needed – to really understand and see what leadership under pressure took and how it can change and save lives."

The back story

"I've just got to get the job done" – or at least that is what I was telling myself.

I was rushing a job, that I didn't need to rush. It just wasn't that urgent. And it was only a five-minute job. I was a young sparky, trying to impress. In short, I was trying to save five minutes.

In saving five minutes I got to go home from hospital five weeks later. A switchboard blew up in my face. BOOM. I spent more than a month in the intensive care and burns units.

I made a silly decision; due to the stress and the pressure that I put on myself. But why? Because I was trying to do a good job. Faster than I needed to. And I wanted to look good and get praise for it. I got scared to work as a sparky. I still am, now.

Fast forward 10 years, and I found myself in a much more stressful role. I was now the Maintenance superintendent in a smelter and working for someone who couldn't control their emotions. Every time the job became stressful; this person verbally exploded. They were abrupt, aggressive, and even abusive. And apparently that was OK. Everyone else tolerated it. So, I had to, too. He had a high stress job, right?

Flying off the handle was considered business as usual. But, for me, it always hurt to be yelled at and I never really understood how stress is reason enough to hurt other humans. This was an example of how not to lead under pressure.

On May 25, 2021, I was on an industrial site that had a major event. Explosions went off at the plant - literally. People feared for their lives or those of their colleagues. Observing how well the response to that incident was managed, completely changed my life and my approach to leadership.

The site leaders stepped up. They stayed in control of their emotions and the situation. They had the courage to make tough decisions, and they cared about the hundreds of people that were affected. It was quite profound to watch the manager and CEO take charge, take control, and take care.

This was an example of how to lead under pressure. That CEO demonstrated how and why strong leadership under pressure is so important. And, how to execute these skills well. That experience taught me what I had failed to learn in the first thirty years of my career. Under pressure leadership is about emotional and situational control – aka: creating CONSCIOUS CONTROL. It is about caring for people, and it is about courageous decision making.

The unpacked story

In general terms, I have been very blessed in life. A lot of the possible tragedies of life have not befallen myself, or my immediate family. And for that, I am grateful. There have been the obligatory challenges faced along the way, but none more than the three listed above. Oh, and one hundred days of anxiety, when a very successful business fell over. But that is another story, and one that Mrs Guinea probably tells better than I do. Apparently being married to an entrepreneur is a roller coaster ride. On reflection though, I would probably still be an electrician in a factory or an industrial site somewhere if I didn't have that switchboard incident at the age twenty-one.

It is now interesting to look back on that experience, with more knowledge about the human psyche and some insights into why we do what we do (I have since studied Psychology). In short, we put pressure on ourselves to look good. To be better. To get praised for doing a good job. Or for doing a quick job. Instead of doing the job properly and safely. Daniel Kahneman (2011) stated, "decision making, particularly when we are under pressure, is a priority quandary." Winning the Nobel Prize in 2002 for his work on the psychology of good decision-making. He also details an interesting view of the brain in his book, Thinking Fast and Slow (2011), suggesting when it comes to decision making we have two distinct decisions making systems.

System 1 operates automatically and quickly, with little or no effort, and no sense of voluntary control (for example when we detect emotions in others or when we brush our teeth in the morning).

System 2 requires attention for the high effort mental activities that demand it, including complex computations. This system is often associated with the subjective experience of actions, choice, and concentration.

In short, I used a steel ruler to measure where we were going to mount something in a switchboard. Crazy. And I knew better, that is the worst part. If I was able to control my excitement (and emotions), things might have been different. Hindsight is wonderful. I was very much operating with system 1, where I should have been operating at system 2. I gave myself permission to rush. To risk - life and limb. It was a decision that resulted in five weeks of recovery; firstly, in intensive care, then the burn's unit in Brisbane with 15% of my body covered in second degree burns.

And if you have ever been to a burn's unit, you will know that they are some of the saddest places on earth. The screams, the smells, and the shattered humans - some who don't leave alive - stay in your memory forever. The nurses are amazing. I always wondered if they ever experience compassion overload and get sick of forcibly removing skin or wiping bums. They never seemed to, and it was a credit to them. Mind you, I will say, with love, that no-one wipes your bum quite like you do. True story.

The morning routine was a bath - getting naked – remember I couldn't use my hands. Then, a toilet trip with a wonderful and patient nurse. Followed by the suppository – also with a wonderful and patient nurse. Then, the debriding; aka, skin being forcibly removed from my face and hands. Each morning for about five weeks. All because I put pressure on myself to rush and risk. I had put my job before myself. The saddest part of being injured at such a young age was that I didn't really have the coping skills to deal with the situation. I wasn't yet resilient. Lying in the burn's unit, it was all woe me.

And why me? Yes, eventually, I looked around and realised that I wasn't actually burnt that badly. In the scheme of things, that was.

And suddenly, I was afraid of electricity. And if I was scared of electricity, how could I work in this trade that I had studied and practiced for the past four years? Eventually, I did find work as an electrician, but I had committed to myself (whilst lying in the burn's unit) that I would find another career, and something else to do.

After massive reflection following the incident, I have come to understand that the pressure we put on ourselves can lead us to making careless or even life-threatening decisions. It is important to be self-aware enough to know when this is happening so that you can change your behaviour and not let the pressure win.

A week or two before the incident, I had applied for a job on a mine site in WA. During my recovery, that mine site rang my family (on a land line phone), who rang the burn's unit, to pass on a message that they wanted to interview me on the day I was released back into the world. And they did. The interview went well, and I got the job.

I worked as an Electrician for three long years, before I could get off the tools. I got promoted into a technical role. I was twenty-four and am forever grateful for the senior leaders that gave me the opportunity. Because I couldn't talk about the incident, they didn't know my back story.

I was ashamed and embarrassed about what had happened. No-one knew. I hadn't processed it, and I couldn't share that I was scared every time I went near electricity.

For ten years following that incident, Mrs G and I worked in several different states and one territory, while I attempted to climb the ladder of corporate success. This was going well, and I climbed to the middle level leadership ranks of Maintenance Superintendent, which meant that I was then in charge of more than one team, and more than one leader. It was an extremely stressful role, and one that required huge hours on site. I was working in a smelter, and the equipment was old and unreliable. It used to break all the time, and I was responsible for both trying to keep it running and responding to and repairing the failures when they occurred. And they did. I didn't cope with the pressure of that role very well at all. And nor did the senior leaders that I reported to. One of the senior leaders was a loose cannon. Whenever the pressure came on, he went ballistic. Nuts. Screaming and shouting at his teams, and his people. He had zero self-control. Zero emotional control. He made it ok to berate staff members. To belittle them, in front of others. To beat them up emotionally. And it never felt good to get yelled at. It hurt a lot. And I could never understand why it was ok to treat people like that. Maybe because it is something that I would never think about doing to people in my team. Ever. But it was alright in that workplace. It was accepted as the workplace culture. I know I was damaged. I was knocked about, big time. It was time to start reflecting again. Instead of being a victim, I started thinking about how I felt when I was treated poorly by a leader, and what I could do about helping leaders to understand that their behaviour can leave a lasting impact on people – either positively, or in this case, negatively. I wasn't sure at that stage what the answer was or how to help leaders and their teams.

Not long after that experience, we relocated to our hometown of Gladstone, Queensland. Although I hadn't talked about the switchboard incident for the previous ten years, I had to now. People kept asking about it; if I was ok? What had happened? How was I coping?

I gained a job on an Alumina Refinery, that was being constructed and commissioned at the time. Part of the induction process involved watching a video featuring someone called Charlie Morecraft. Charlie had been burnt on an industrial site, and talked about his survival, and the impacts of the incident on him and his family which were significant. Over 50% of Charlie's body was burnt and he was given his last rights. But he was a survivor, soon changing his career to become a Safety Speaker. That sounds interesting, was my first thought. I was moved by the video and Charlie's ability to tell his story and engage people in his learnings.

Not long after that I got asked to chair a safety meeting. I decided to tell my switchboard story. I showed the photos of me, and talked about the whole experience, including my learnings. "It happened to me; it might happen to you." I shared with the audience who seemed to like the story and the presentation. Then, six months later, I got the chance to deliver the presentation again. I loved it that much, I handed in my resignation and told my leader that I was quitting to become a 'safety speaker', like Charlie, which made for an interesting discussion when I arrived at home that evening. Without a job. With two little boys. And a wife who wasn't working at the

time. And a mortgage. Apparently, I was not acting like a grownup - thanks for the gift of feedback, Mrs G., love ya.

Having no idea what I was doing, my career as a Safety Speaker began. I knew I could help others stay safe. Very soon after I started sharing my story with teams around Australia and internationally, leaders started asking me about how to be better safety leaders; aka, how to lead the safety process, especially during pressure times, when budgets or schedules were tight. This became my next job. Working with leaders to help them develop safe teams.

Then, on May 25, 2021, my world changed forever. I was on an industrial site, doing leadership and team development work, when the site went BOOM – literally. There was a major equipment failure not far from where I was sitting which could have been catastrophic if anyone was injured. What I saw happen next was nothing short of amazing. The site management team stepped up. They took control, they were in care factor mode. We didn't know at the time that no-one had been injured and they made the decisions that needed to be made swiftly and calmly.

It was a scary time. There was a lot happening. There were two hundred plus people needing to be updated and needing to know what was happening. We were safely and caringly moved from the site to the town office, where the managers could address all staff. This was done in a professional and positive way with an understand of the stress that people were under. We were assured that the site was being made safe, that no-one was injured, that the management team were working hard to understand how to respond, and that we should head home or to a hotel provided and reconvene back there at 8 am. Again, in the morning, we were updated in a caring and compassionate way. The company CEO had flown into town the night before. The way the CEO and management team took charge of the situation was the best I have ever seen. Or felt.

It was quite amazing to hear the managers and the CEO focus on the people on site and put them first. There was a real sense of we know what you are going through and are here to support type of approach to the communications from the senior leaders. One example of that was the fact that every single person had left the site in a hurry and had to evacuate without any of their personal effects. Everything was on site. Everything. Phone.

Keys. Wallet. Computer. All we were left with was what we were wearing. Literally. I was actually quite amazed at how much stress this put on me, and the other people involved. It was quite uncomfortable not having any of my personal belongings, or access to my car. It was weird.

And those leaders managed to stay in control and keep their emotions in check. Which meant that they could keep their behaviour in check and keep the situation in control. They demonstrated care factor for the people and teams involved, and they made courageous decisions. Both in the moment, and in the days following the incident.

The current story

My whole world shifted, particularly after the experience on the site in May 2021. It was a powerful lightbulb moment where I finally realised the missing piece that was needed to really understand and see what leadership under pressure took - how it can not only change lives but save lives.

Although most of my effort since I have been in business has been around working with leaders in pressure situations, like safety and keeping people physically and psychologically safe at work, not long after May 2021, our business transformed itself into a business that continually and relentlessly asks the question, "Why is it important for leaders to stay calmer and more controlled under pressure, and how can we help them to do that?"

It changed my world so much that I am currently enrolled in a Master of Research, to study and research that question, and to really unpack how I can take what I have learnt through the years and share that information with leaders.

In summary:

Pressure does funny things. It starts with sweaty palms, shaky voices, noisy minds. And too often ends with bad decisions and dangerous errors.

But the thing about pressure is often there's no danger, but our body believes there is. So, we freeze – physically, mentally, emotionally. And no matter how hard we try; we can't take back control.

I've been in these situations myself. At twenty-one, an error in a high-pressure environment almost cost me my life. But thankfully, instead, it put me on a different path.

Since then, I've worked with hundreds of teams and hundreds of leaders to answer the question: How can we stay calm and controlled whilst under pressure?

You see, dealing with pressure is a skill you were probably never taught. Either at school, at home, or in the workplace. Most of the time it's a skill we don't even realise we need.

But I've discovered there are ways to develop it:

Ways to make great decisions under pressure.

Ways to become the leader that others aspire to be like.

Ways for teams to come together, no matter the situation.

What we need to do is to elevate our decision-making abilities, and to live and lead consciously under pressure. Equipped with under pressure skills, we unfreeze when the pressure is on.

Freeing our body and mind so we can take control, we can care for others, and make the best decisions in any situation.

www.theguineagroup.com.au

BRAD BURCHNELL

FINDING HOPE AFTER MY DAUGHTER'S SUICIDE
IN HONOUR OF BEVERLEY

"Despite my survivor's guilt, I finally felt free and able to restore my joy and choose my own happiness and to own it. I realised that it's no one's responsibility other than mine to make me happy. That's what Bev would have wanted for me."

While I have shared this story with my therapist, friends, family and with my girlfriend, I have never written it out in full. I will preface it with this, it is written with loving care, honour to her, and for those struggling with the loss of a loved one and for you to know, that there is hope on the other side.

Beverly was born in the early morning hours of April 22, 1981, on Earth Day as she would fondly tell me often years later. She was blond, bubbly, and sweet. She was my study buddy. I was a young father going to college on the GI Bill after active duty in the U.S. Navy, working three part time jobs. She would sit on her daddy's lap as she hated being apart from me. Her Mom worked nights and we struggled in our marriage and separated after two years. That's where I believe her mental health issues began. as I did my best to reassure her of my love for her and how it was better for her mom and I to be friends rather than arguing as we had been for many years. After two years of separation, we divorced. Beverly and I spent as much time together as possible. While I was living in Redondo Beach, CA we would go to the beach, make sandcastles, fly kites and just be happy. She was a beach baby and lover of the sun. I remarried in 1988 and had two other daughters Elizabeth and Emily all of whom were thick as thieves together and she loved being the oldest and doted on her little sisters. While with us she had chores like any normal household and helped her baby sisters do theirs. She read to them, played with them and loved them beyond measure. It was amazing. As time went on and they all grew, challenges began popping up as work dried up in Southern California and we had to move due to job opportunities first in Colorado and then to SE Michigan. My philosophy was to be no different with any of my kids when we were all together or apart. My expectation was for her to mind her Mom and respect her when I was not there. When Bev was with us, she had responsibilities and behaviour expectations. I had really no idea what was going on in her home with her Mom or what she was experiencing. She was a latch key kid in a small town in Central California. She was amazing in what I knew of her and from what she told me. My fondest memory was when she was sixteen and she and I were out and about together in my car. She looked at me and asked, "Hey Dad, are you hungry?" This was Bev speak for I'm hungry. I asked where she thought I might like to eat at and we ended up at a place called Fosters Freeze for a burger, fries and shake. It was a wonderful day and one that lights up my heart. Only second to that was when I asked her when she got married if I would be the one to walk her down the aisle. She was my princess and it was something I still remember. She said of course and that I was her Dad and she loved me, who else would walk her down the aisle?

Graduation day from High School summer 2000. I watched with pride as my sweet beautiful daughter graduated full of promise with a plan to go off to San Diego State to study Psychology. The day after was somewhat foreboding as her Mom left with her step sister and husband to move to Utah with them. Leaving Bev behind to finish cleaning and ready to vacate the apartment. She was not ready for that overwhelming experience and my Mom and I worked with her to get it addressed. We got it all settled and sorted including acquiring storage for anything she wouldn't need as she was house sitting for the summer. Last step was arranging for her to get food for the house she was watching.

She entered University and flourished in the area and did very well including becoming a Montessori teacher where I had the pleasure of watching her in action, she was in control and very much in her element as she loved children, and they adored her. She was a kid magnet and baby whisperer. She reveled in the experience including a study trip abroad in Chile. She experienced a new culture, new food and new family. She graduated in May 2004 with her Bachelor's Degree in Psychology. The next step was her Master's so she could become licensed to practice in the State. She moved through her classes and we talked a great deal as I was also going through a similar program and we compared notes about our different classes and approaches to mental health and helping others. At a certain point there is a requirement for all Master's candidates to participate in their Practicum (Residency for Psychological professionals). She was provided three choices:

1. Work with teenage girls at risk and given her loving nature and experiences I thought this was a perfect vehicle for her professional development.

2. Work with one of her professors who was a clinician in the area of Marriage and Family Therapy which was one of her areas of election.

3. Art therapy for Pediatric Hospice - this frightened me greatly as I had friends working with hospice patients and also my experience watching my father over a six-month period fade until his death in December 1980. Bev had a penchant for connection and empathy deeply. I shared my fears and asked her if she was prepared to lose patients? She said she was and that she could handle it. I strongly urged her not to go that direction. She misunderstood my fears and took it as a gauntlet that I had thrown down and that I didn't think she could do it (as found out later). She took this step and entered in anyway.

In 2007 she dropped out of her Master's class and began to destabilize noticeably. Her appearance became thinner, and more gaunt than she had appeared from the last visit, her alcohol consumption intake was more than I had seen previously. It became apparent she had an eating disorder and as I found out later, she had been struggling with that illness since her Senior Year in High School.

She asked if she could come home to Michigan and live with us. I told her that I would need to speak to the family and discuss everything. We came up with a game plan and the room for her to move in. The plan included finding her a job, getting her a car and for her to go to therapy which I would pay for as I had already met with a therapist. The next day I talked to her and laid out the plan, she said thank you but she would be moving to Wasilla, Alaska to live with her oldest half-sister. It ended up being a disaster with multiple calls from her about hating it there, crying, and telling me she wanted to die. I had to ask if she was serious or was it a turn of phrase, and if it was that she wanted to do harm to herself, then I would have to take action. Hindsight is so 20/20.

This began my downward spiral in my marriage and relationship with my kids as I felt I needed to defend my daughter and interactions with my wife began to take on interrogations. I began to shut down and actively began to disconnect from friends and my family.

Bev began to run in a fashion, she moved back with her Mom in a small Central California town and then moved in with a man. I wasn't thrilled with her cohabitation as I know the statistics of relationships working or not working after marriage. That Christmas was happy, and we had a great time. She looked lovely and the conversation, food and fun was wonderful. The following year we went to California to celebrate as a family again. This time it was dramatically different. She looked disheveled, noticeably inebriated, and belligerent towards everyone. She wanted to fight and argue that night. The only thing that I can relate it to would be that of the movie the Exorcist or the Omen. It was such a palpable evil presence, and her behaviour was so bad that we picked up and left. We found out later that she had briefly been in AA and had been struggling with drugs and alcohol.

Things continued to go from bad to worse, running to Missouri to work at a gym owned by a friend from High School, and lived at a house he owned with his sister, The sister left and the utilities had to be turned off in order to force her out. She returned to Central California and then ultimately back to San Diego, CA where she loved the area, and felt the most at peace but, on the other hand, she was finding none of it. She called and asked once again to come back to Michigan to live and I told her no and that I would support her to receive therapy and that I would foot the bills, but she needed to stop running, plant her feet, and face the reasons she was running from herself. I didn't want to enable her.

The next day she took a trip up to Big Bear to spend in the mountains. She took several bottles of wine and in a state of depression aimed her car while coming back down on the freeway to a solid wall in attempt to take her life. She crashed her mini cooper head on. This was the first attempt in Jan – Feb, 2016.

She was placed into hospital in Loma Linda ICU and was on a ventilator for several days. She did come out of it. Lost a great deal of blood, had lots of internal injuries and an open wound that was never repaired even at the time of her ultimate death. In 2017 while at the home of a friend of her mother's she was found in a pool with weights and a knife. She was taken to hospital for observation as she had injured her neck causing her to have stainless steel pins put in her neck. Her open wound was still present, and she constantly had prescription painkillers always with her.

She came out for her sister's wedding, but was in no physical condition to attend and we had to make the difficult decision to not allow her to attend. The result was devastating for everyone. She was sent back early as she needed to be at a place that could care for her, so she ultimately went to live with her Mom in a nine-story senior apartment building. As they had done previously her Mom, Bev, and some friends had planned to watch the sunset on top of the roof and enjoy orange and root beer floats. Her Mom asked Bev if she could go down to the soda machine located at the bottom of the stairs and get the drinks. She responded to her mom saying, it was going to take her a long enough time just to get to the roof. So, on that day, May 28, 2018, my sweet girl took a leap off the roof of the apartment building and ended her life.

My whole world changed. It was my job to protect her, and the survivor's guilt was overwhelming and the shame of being the Dad who couldn't protect his daughter from herself was a huge weight that was magnifying other childhood trauma that I had never addressed when as a child or teenager. I finally agreed to go to counselling. I was in such deep pain and had walled myself off. My marriage and relationship with my spouse had over the years drifted due to neglect between us both, but I was in such emotional pain, turmoil and lacking the appearance of emotional support that I reached out to other women for emotional needs online, but no physical affairs. However, the damage was discovered, and divorce was initiated by my spouse. I own that and don't excuse the behaviour. I avoided the most difficult conversations, the hard ones that were about our relationship, and the voids and hurts within it. My fears, shame, and guilt were overwhelming me, and I just choked everything down and it hurt a great number of people. Most of all my kids.

In 2019 I left my home of twenty years with a heaviness that I had not experienced previously, just before my birthday, and Thanksgiving of 2019. I went into the unknown - an emotional and mental mess. I found a new therapist as my previous one had displayed what I termed as less than a clinical approach towards me and felt it unprofessional. Now with a new therapist, I began to unravel me, still not getting to the core and root of my trauma and its depth. I was diagnosed with PTSD not from the military, but a prolonged trauma due to my daughter's struggles and death, along with my own childhood and adolescent trauma. The helps available today were not available in my time nor were such things really talked about. Especially not with me specifically. We were taught not to cry, to deal with it, shake it off, dust yourself off, and move on. I was able to take two months of paid FMLA (Medical Leave) to address all of this and concentrate on my mental and emotional health. It's been a great blessing.

My lightbulb moment, however, wasn't truly realised until after I had undertaken a seven-month intensive self-examination programme called the 'BREATH' framework. It encompasses evaluating who you are at your beginning, identifying what or who you have given power over you, examining your core values, going deep into behaviors attachment issues, trauma and pain while engaging in one of the most cathartic processes ever, writing letters of forgiveness to yourself and those involved. By doing this, I was able to lay those things down forever, bringing me a great sense of peace and healing. I gave up any numbing agents like alcohol along with dating. One day having gone through each segment of this healing process, I had a defining lightbulb moment where I realised that others might benefit what I had learned and experienced. Sharing it with others about what I had experienced might be the last step in my healing journey. It also struck me that up to this point I had continued in my life to be selfish and that moving forward I wished to be more selfless by providing to others. By doing this it has enabled me to lay down my pain and trauma and find the peace that I wish for others.

While not everything is right as rain, I've discovered a great deal on my journey. I have a great group of men that are closer to me than brothers because of shared traumas through a group founded by Traver Boehm called, The UNcivilized Nation. They are an International, Regional, and Local based group of men that address issues affecting men's unique mental and emotional growth needs. We are able to share with each other openly and know we are no longer alone. We hold space for one another. We have ongoing zoom calls, meetings, communication methods to encourage and communicate. I finally feel free and able to restore my joy and choose my own happiness and to own it. It's no one's responsibility other than mine to make me happy.

I have constructed a solid approach with my therapist and physician who uses a holistic approach to medicine and a fitness/nutrition coach and the last for me is to find the right spiritual venue to grow as well. I've chosen to live openly, honestly, genuinely, with full transparency and owning my life. I've committed to share my entire story with any woman that I would seek as a long-term love partner, and I have done that. I have shared with her every aspect and have vowed never to hurt another woman the way that I did my previous spouse. I would act honorably, have the hard conversations, not argue, not belittle nor lash out, but rather to communicate and seek understanding. That's my commitment that I have made to her too.

I concentrate on growing each day to become a good man and not a nice guy. A nice guy is someone who seeks what is best for himself and acts out with self-sabotaging behaviors. I don't have it all figured out yet and doubt that I will fully, but I know that my job is to contribute towards other's happiness, serve others fully, and use the knowledge that I have gained through my own failures to help other men avoid the pitfalls and minefields that I have laid for myself. Being a victim is limiting and living a life of liberty is a beautiful thing. I will have to make a great many amends to people over time and the first will be to my daughters. I can't control when or how our relationships will be reconstructed, but I have to be prepared for the fact that maybe they might not want one and that is their decision and one that is valid for them. Some of the strategies I would like to share with you that have helped me greatly on my journey are the following:

1. Accept you for you

2. Love yourself first and best so that you might love others fully and well

3. Live life honestly with transparency

4. Seek understanding to be understood

5. Challenge your mindset

6. Don't do it alone you can't overcome as you will be overcome

7. Don't seek others validation, but rather your own

8. Seek your own worth because you are worthy, worthy of love, friendship, renewal, restoration, acceptance, grace and forgiveness

9. Never seek your own way but find a band of like-minded others that will challenge you - physically, mentally, educationally and spiritually

10. Understand and accept that you are not going to be able to control the outcome of others. You only have control of you.

11. Last, look in the mirror and tell yourself four notable qualities that are worthy about you and do it daily

My wish to whomever reads this, that they are encouraged and can embrace the same changes. It is a daily act of intention towards change. It's worth it!

BRAD BURCHNELL – LIFE COACH FROM MY HEART TO YOURS LLC – Author

www.fmhtyllc.com

CRAIG HUMBLE

A DEVASTATED DAD
FINDING LIFE IN A JAIL CELL

"Jail was a real turning point in my life 'for the better'. In the first month of my jail term, I met a salvation Army chaplain who changed my life forever."

These days, I am a business owner. I live a stable wonderful life and am a dad of five wonderful kids. I love motorbikes and investing hope into my local community, but it wasn't always that way.

I grew up in a normal household, the son of a policeman. My dad went on to open a few businesses after leaving the force and I think that's where my entrepreneurial gifts have come from. I started going out with my ex-wife when I was fifteen and she fell pregnant when I was seventeen and we were married as soon as I turned eighteen. After my first son was born twenty months later we had a second child together. I was working two jobs which meant I wasn't home a lot. Being young, I thought the best thing I could do was work and provide for my family and when I wasn't working I still liked to catch up with my mates, so I do take some responsibility for the next stage in my life. Nevertheless, I was gutted the day I went out to work and came home to an empty house. I later realised my wife had been having an affair for some time with her stepbrother that lived in Victoria and that she was a heroin addict. I tried to contact her on numerous occasions, but she made it very hard and avoided all contact.

My family didn't like my ex-wife a great deal and as much as I was concerned about my kids we decided to just give up trying to make contact for now as it was taking a great toll on me emotionally. About a year later, I met another girl and we hit it off, deciding to travel around for a while. We bought a 4-wheel drive and a camper trailer and set off on our travels. We travelled the east coast stopping in Port Macquarie. I snagged a job in a night club because we were there one night and a fight broke out which I quickly broke up, holding one of the guys until security came, so they offered me a job. I was employed as a bar man and then promoted to bar manager and then onto club manager. This led to us selling the camper van and moving into a unit as we felt settled in Port Macquarie. My current girlfriend had cheated on me a few times at this stage, but I stayed with her because I felt I really couldn't do any better.

Then one night at the club, I had a sliding doors moment where I met my now wife Jodie through one of the girls that worked for me. One of the first things I said to her was. "I have two kids and I want them to be a part of my life." She was keen and I broke it off with the girlfriend I currently had and started to date Jodie. I knew there was something special about her. She was different to all the other girls that were at the club. Jodie had grown up in a Christian home and had a whole different take on life than what I was used to. We really got on well and I felt a strong connection straight away. We moved in together and were married within two years. Jodie fell pregnant with our first child Maddison, then we made the decision together to embark on finding my kids.

When we finally made contact I shockingly and very sadly discovered through the authorities that my eldest boy had been abused in every way possible by his stepfather. There were no words to express how hard this news was to take. I felt like I had let my boys down and hadn't protected them. Even though it wasn't my fault I couldn't stop feeling like it was. After many long trips driving to Melbourne for family court appearances and meetings with the Department of Human Services, I finally got to see to my two boys for the first time in forever on a supervised visit.

I was pretty excited because the next visit was going to be an overnight visit with my boys, and we could do some activities and get the chance to rebuild our relationship. I took down a few pushbikes for the boys and a play station for them as gifts. We had a great weekend together and they were full of questions and generally excited to have contact with me. I drove the twelve hour trip back home after dropping them off and was looking forward to seeing them again in a month for another overnight adventure. When that time came around and I tried to make contact with them to arrange a pickup time, I could not get in contact with them. I called the Department of Human Services who did a welfare visit and found the home empty.

The next phone call I received was from Melbourne CIB stating I was required to attend Dandenong Police Station in relation to allegations of assault against my boys. What? I had to drive twelve hours to Victoria to be interviewed about allegations I had sexually abused my eldest boy during my only contact visit with them in over four years, this was to be one of the hardest days I had ever faced. After the interrogation the police informed me that the interview was procedure only and that the stepfather was going to be charged with sexually assaulting my son.

At this time, I was hanging out with an outlaw motorcycle club and was helping them on weekends with DJ's for their parties and bringing people to their clubhouse after the night club had shut for the night. In my desperation, I spoke with a friend who was a member of the club, and they said, "this guy needs to be taken care of" and in the state of shock and grief I was in, I agreed. I asked if he could help me with that and we set a plan for it to occur. But before the stepfather could be charged or taken care of by my friends, I discovered he had taken his own life by suicide in the family home. When I look back now had he not ended his own life, I could and most definitely would have been charged if anything had happened to him on my account.

Not long after, we got a call from the Department of Human Services stating that my ex-wife was not coping with my eldest boy and was going to give him up so we quickly applied for a custody order and were awarded six months interim custody of my eldest son and my younger son stayed with his foster family which he had grown up with. After a few months we came to realise that not only was my son physically damaged, but he was also very emotionally traumatised. We sought treatment for him, and he ended up needing surgery on one of his eye muscles because he had been beaten so hard his eyes were turned in a different direction. We also sought counselling to work through everything he had been through. Our daughter was young also and due to my son's sexual abuse my wife felt it was not safe to have him living in the same house. He didn't do anything and didn't try anything, but my wife felt strongly that it wouldn't be wise.

This was a huge turning point in my life - Do I make the decision to give up my son I had just found, or do I lose my marriage and daughter? I made the best decision I could at the time, to send him to his maternal grandmother's house in Queensland. This didn't last long; he kept running away, breaking stuff and being physically aggressive with her. As a result, I received a call from the Department of Child Services in Queensland who informed me if I did not take him back they would make him a ward of the state and I would lose all rights to him. Standing at a crossroad and not knowing what to do, I called my Dad who was an ex-policeman and asked if they could possibly take my son in and try to help him. He agreed. I drove to Brisbane airport where I was met by the Department of Community Services Queensland. They handed over my son with some pills and said, "if he gets noisy just give him these." This was such a hard trip home seeing him in this state, and all because of what adults had done to him, including me I thought. All he really wanted and deserved was to be loved not to be used or thrown away like a problem that can't be fixed.

My mum and dad met me at Port Macquarie and took my son with them, but sadly they experienced the same. Dad was hit, windows broken, and he kept running away. Eventually, I had to make the very hard, and at the time devastating decision, to make my son a ward of the state in New South Wales. He went into a group home situation which (in the long term was the best thing for him) but I struggled so hard making this decision. I felt like I had failed as a dad, and I think that was one of the most difficult decisions to make and come to terms with. I had no friends at the time that I could talk to about how I was feeling, and I think that played a huge part in in what led me to make the following fateful life choices that were to follow.

The fact that I had worked in a night club and associated with an outlaw motorcycle club helping them with their club nights providing DJ's and entertainment, gave me easy access to drugs. Something I had never touched up until that point. I was not coping with life at all and was filled with anger and remorse about what had happened to my sons. In order to escape the pain, I began taking drugs, and next thing I knew I was dealing and taking up to fifteen ecstasy tablets a day. Shortly after, I was arrested by the Tactical Response Team along with six other co-offenders in an operation across Sydney and the Mid North coast after dealing to an undercover cop. My wife was also arrested for knowingly taking part in the supply of a prohibited drug. I was held on remand for eleven months in maximum security before being sentenced to four years nine months. My wife was given two hundred hours community service for her charges.

Jail was a real turning point in my life 'for the better'. In the first month of my jail term, I met a Salvation Army chaplain. One day he told me about the Christian faith and that there was a different way to live. This was the lightbulb moment that turned my life in a whole different direction. Especially when he told me there was a free gift of Forgiveness and wholeness available to me through Jesus Christ. He gave me a Bible and helped me understand what it all meant. I made a decision to accept Jesus into my life and I instantly felt released from all the bad things I had done throughout my life, and I felt like I had a new opportunity to start afresh. Filled with anticipation for the future, I was a changed man, and I went on to lead many other prisoners to the Lord while I was in jail as they could see there was joy and hope in my life even though I was in a jail cell doing time.

During my time in prison, Jodie met some amazing people on the outside that owned a small network communications mobile phone shop. They became my weekend leave sponsors when I was in my last six months of my jail term and when I was released they also employed me in their shop which was a real blessing as it started me on my journey with the mobile phone business - Network Communications. My friends decided to sell their shop and I was given the opportunity to buy their business. But first, I had to meet with Mike Jeffs the founder and CEO of

Network Communications before I could be approved to purchase the business. He was also a Christian, knew about my past and knew my story, and still he was happy to give me the opportunity to own the business and have an amazing fresh start to become the owner of my own business which meant I could provide for my family.

We owned that store for about twelve months and the opportunity came up to purchase a second store in the Hunter Valley and we took that opportunity and then went on to buy another four stores in our time with Network Communications which spanned over sixteen years. Network communications also fund the Australian Christian Channel and give to so many charities around the world and that's what I really loved. Being a part of something bigger with a purpose.

In December 2019 we sold our stores and bought Black Market Espresso bar in Mooloolaba which was a run-down little place which I rebuilt turning it into a thriving Espresso Bar that was rated Number one in Mooloolaba for coffee by many websites and product review apps. We built it on good old customer service, hard work and absolute excellence and attention to details when it came to coffee. I know how important it is in business to do the big thing well and don't let the little things distract you from your purpose, which in our business was to have the best coffee. We built the business from 5kg of coffee a week to well over 50kg in our peak times. We sold that business in December 2021 for a healthy profit which enabled me to start my Real estate journey.

I have just opened my own Buyers Agent business on the Sunshine Coast and I'm really enjoying the business so much as it is all about helping people. I get to hear their stories, their dreams and help them fulfill those dreams, as we source out their investment property, dream home or beach house. What I have learnt in life is that we are our biggest limiter to what we can achieve. I brought my first mobile phone shop with a credit card; I was given a chance because a CEO could see a genuine love for God in my life but also a genuine change from the person I use to be. We need to be willing to take risks, believe in ourselves and step out of the past that may be holding us back. I have so much from my past that could take hold of me, but I made a choice one day, in a jail cell to change, to forgive myself, to allow myself to dream that there is more to life and not let my past control me or my future.

When I left jail I knew this for sure, I wanted to serve the Lord and give back to the community and share my story of everything I had been through and more importantly thrived through so that other people would have hope for their life also. I met an amazing man who was the president of the Christian Sport Bike Association, we served together for six years and then he went on to be the Chaplain for the Australian superbikes and I stepped up to the president role. I have been totally blessed since leaving jail with many successful businesses and friendships, but the biggest blessings are my family and God.

CRAIG HUMBLE - MOTOR BIKE ENTHUSIAST - REAL ESTATE BUYERS AGENT

Craighumble777@gmail.com

DAVID STEWART

LIFE AFTER ADDICTION
THE COMPASSIONATE LEADER HELPING
OTHERS FIND HOPE

"I decided I'd have a go at recovery. I gave in to what people call my disease. I put down my gun and took off my body armour. I stepped out from behind the nets. It was May 7, 1998, and I haven't had a drink of alcohol since that ugly night. It's been over 23 years."

This is my life journey. The memory of my past. Not a separate life or an old life, but my life. My own imprint. My family DNA. The blood I spilled in order to change. The damage I choose to leave in the past by living in the present. The legacies of love I decided to open and claim. I offer this to you, my sons. Not a house or cars or careers, but a father's life gift. An open letter. His life. His mistakes. His lessons. The life he has walked.

My gorgeous boys, I am flawed, and I took my flaws into fatherhood. Know that my intentions have always been true. I have never made a choice with an agenda other than love. My life journey commenced with hope and innocence, but naiveté is not an excuse. Ultimately, I hope it helps you understand me with a bit more clarity and kindness.

Even in my recovery, I have made mistakes and acted in self-pity, grandiosity, and denial. I am sorry, and I will always continue to make right what I made wrong. What is wrong can't always be made right. Thank you for loving me. I feel humbled by your courage and forgiveness. What I have done is admit and own my vulnerability and humanity. I gave up making excuses and accepted that all we have is today. One day, one life.

Somewhat ironically (for both the church and myself), I was born in Sydney on November 1, 1961. In Catholic speak, this is a holy day of obligation known as All Saints' Day. I am a man of good intentions (maybe), but a saint? Definitely not! I had a bad streak in me that ended up running its course until my thirty-sixth year on this wondrous, destructive planet. I have learned by error after error that the wonder of the earth never leaves us. Rather, we just choose to leave the wonder. Destruction Is a negative possibility created by the wrong choices.

Life in the Sydney suburbs of the 1960s was basic but good. Milk was delivered in bottles, and garbage was collected twice a week in one steel, circular bin. Kids played on the street, and the front door was always open. Neighbours talked to each other over the back fences, and dog leashes didn't exist (we also didn't have dogs who mauled children). Simple blessings. We went to church on Sunday morning and the local Chinese restaurant on Friday night. When it was hot, we sat under a sprinkler. When it was cold, we put on a woollen jumper. Simple pleasures.

As my father's political and business careers blossomed, I moved from Punchbowl to Cronulla to the harbour suburb of Vaucluse with my kind and beautiful mother and my two sisters. We followed Dad. He was head of the house; no questions were asked or answered. As a point-of-suburb reference, Punchbowl was a working-class, stinking-hot melting pot of cultures and cuisines; Cronulla was a right wing, middle-class mecca filled with beaches, golf courses, strong cars, and even stronger opinions; and Vaucluse was awash with private schools, three-level corporate retreats, boats, and black BMWs—and wankers. I was full of all of the above, and I mean full of it!

As our family homes and cars got bigger, so did my ego and sensitivity. In 1976, at the age of fourteen, I was lucky enough to be sent to Waverley College, the Christian brothers' leading educational light for schoolboys in Sydney. It was (and is) an amazing school. We competed against the elite boys of Sydney's private schools. We didn't really belong. Waverley boys had a brash aggression that other private school boys lacked. We had no time for airs, graces, and political correctness. Our fathers were lawyers, businessmen, criminals, publicans, tradesmen, shopkeepers, farmers, sportsmen, and surfers. We rejoiced in our differences, and each and every kid was accepted with rebuke followed by open arms.

Waverley playgrounds and sporting fields were not for the faint-hearted; I had my share of conflicts. Good or bad, it was a rite of passage. We hung tight, and we stuck it up every other school that played sport against us. The elite of Sydney's eastern suburbs looked down on us with a plum and aplomb. That antiestablishment attitude stayed with me well into adulthood, and it fuelled a lot of my success (and rebellious behaviour). I thrived on the competition, chaos, and energy it provided and created. I liked to draw a line in the sand and letting go of that need to be right was a major period of positive growth for this flawed man.

From twelve years of age, I showed potential as a cricketer. I opened the bowling as a left hander, batted in the middle order, and fielded with purpose and desire. I loved the game and still do. Cricket is in my blood. At sixteen, after one game in the First Eleven at Waverley, I was selected in the 1978 NSW school boys' carnival and took the most wickets for any opening bowler in that carnival. I had a number of senior coaches and former Australian Test players telling me I was a future star of the game.

At seventeen, I was playing Grade Cricket in the Sydney men's competition and took four wickets in my first game at Parramatta in a first-grade trial game. I had intimidated and out bowled seasoned professionals. I knocked out the middle stump of a batsman who was trying to bully me with gestures and words. As he walked off, I suggested he spend more time in the nets. I may have also reminded him that I was much younger and prettier, and he needed to have a good look in the mirror. My ego was blossoming, but dear God, I felt alive!

At eighteen, I was offered the chance to play in England. It was a great honour, but my dad didn't think it was a great idea. He may have seen through me; at eighteen, I was already driving to cricket games drunk and hung over after leaving Kings Cross nightclubs at six in the morning. I began to miss training, and I found myself talking rubbish and spinning lies in seedy bars. I became an excellent liar, another habit that took years to change.

After not listening to doctors and physiotherapists, I continued to play with a damaged back (the curse of every fast bowler) and did permanent damage to my supple spine. I carry the lumps and aches of stress fractures in my lower back and neck to this day.

By age nineteen, my cricketing career at an elite level was over. I wasn't even a man, and my career was over due to poor decisions fuelled by alcohol abuse. Over! I carried the loss and resentment of that for another twenty years. Addiction had taken away the God-given talent I did not give myself the pleasure of developing. I hadn't even turned twenty, and it was all gone.

I continued to play the game I was born to play well into my forties and was still able to take wickets, catches, and score runs as an aggressive middle-order player, but I was playing on one leg and no spine. I was broken. During this period, I was also completing a degree in economics at the prestigious University of Sydney. It took me an extra six months to complete the standard three-year degree because I thought it would be amusing to write a male-chauvinist paper for a course about the political economy of women. The well-known feminist professor saw it fit to fail my effort. Feminism: one; David: zero.

For me, University was beer, laughs, midnight oil, and co-toilets with pretty girls. Was it fun? Sure! Was it cultivating and educational? Yes, but not in the classical sense. I eventually got the degree—just! At my graduation ceremony, I had a massive hangover. I will be eternally grateful for the Sydney Uni feminists for teaching me an early lesson in humility and for championing the rights of co-toilets.

At seventeen, I also started dating my childhood sweetheart, and we were married at twenty-two. Cath was stunningly beautiful and athletic. Her nickname was 'Legs Eleven'. Cath has great legs. I was a big fan of those legs, and her gorgeous, sweet heart.

Cath gave me everything she could, but I was a boy—a loving, kind, and generous boy, certainly, but also a stupid boy with no control when the lights went on (for me, the lights went on once a week, and I didn't stop until the lights went out). In our first year of marriage, I was already coming home in taxis at dawn. Sitting in the back of those taxis with ripped shirts and a sick gut; I started to develop a real hatred for the man I was becoming. I was hurting the woman I loved.

I loved Cath, but that's the problem with addiction. You confuse and hurt the people you love most, and if you get better, it's an awful burden to carry. For me, you don't completely mend until you own that burden and let it go—and you don't let it go until you realize addiction is a reason and not an excuse.

The disease concept of addiction has its merits and validity, but for some recovering alcoholics, it becomes another way of avoidance. Bad behaviour needs to be owned; we are sick, but our sickness is not an excuse. It is a reason to put our hands up and accept the anger, resentment, and disgust of our loved ones. We deserve every tear and ounce of their vitriol. We don't wallow in self-pity because the remorse of ego can be extremely dangerous for the victimized addict.

Cath and I were married for twenty-one years. We had a house by the sea, a couple of cars, a few holiday units as well as a generation of tears, repeated hurt, and hostile silence. Business was good in those days. As my father, Hollywood Jack, used to say, "Business is good. Just don't admit it to anyone." Jack and his kids built a business together that spanned Australia and Asia. We had accolades and performed heroics, but we also suffered loss.

Amongst the blood, sweat, tears, and multimillion dollar contracts, Dad and I had some fun. Roppongi in Tokyo will never be the same. That grey-headed guy, and his blue-eyed son are crazy. 'Gaijin' Aussie devils! Amongst the loss and let downs were plenty of success, holidays, and laughter.

Cath and I were good together, but I was still a boy—a naughty boy, a sensitive, silly, and damaged boy. The man would go to work, and for five days a week, the sun would shine, and we would make hay together. On day six, out came the horns, and the boy was lost to the ugly belly of Sydney. Cath sat at home talking to her girlfriends, sharing wine, and wondering where the hell the man she married was. He was lost. When he found himself, it was too late. The damage had been done.

We leave legacies in our life. The legacy I left Cath was loss and despair. Cath handled herself with loyalty and class. She gave me more than I deserved, and to the day I die, I will be in her debt. We divorced in our forties. The loss and disgust of the nights I left Cath waiting in our marital bed still haunt me. When I wake at three am on cold, windy mornings, the spectres of my decay and Cath's sweet face still mock me. This never goes away, no matter how much recovery and reflection you embark towards. Only narcissists deny their wreckage while vulnerable. Real human beings admit and own theirs.

Cath and I did many good things together—great things—but our greatest achievements are our three magnificent sons, Matthew, Patrick and Thomas (or Matt, Pat, and Tom). They are big, beautiful, bold, and courageous men. They tower over their mum, and they have hearts of lions. Cath and I are good parents, and our sons are amazing. They love hard and forgive quickly. They have opinions, but they have empathy. They are twice the man I was at their age. I marvel at their wisdom and perception. As small boys, they watched their father submerge and their mother protect, but they grew up with genuine love and care. We didn't fuss, but we were available.

Even in addiction, wonderful things happen. That's the nature of the beast. The good things lull you into unjustified confidence, and just around the corner, addiction kicks you harder. The higher you go, the harder you fall. I'm harder than my sons, but that is hardly a blessing. I've got an edge and a mongrel in me that helped me survive and even thrive, but it also put me in harm's way. I saw many things a man shouldn't see. I did many things a man shouldn't do. I did things that put men in jail and hospitals, and these are the actions and regrets that corrupt your natural goodness. It takes years to heal from such indiscretions. Some people boast and joke about their behaviour in active addiction. I see no point in self-accolades from loss and destruction.

That's not the man I was raised to be, so why should I seek refuge in parody? Glorifying the past and seeking grandiosity in the present are luxuries I can't afford. I've had to learn too many ugly lessons. I'm not being noble, just circumspect. Back to my sons, though: They saved my life. In a cold, dark, and anonymous room in 1997, after a night of debauchery I had participated in hundreds of times previously, I decided I did not want to leave them a legacy of failure and death.

Alone, on a bed of sweat and bodily fluid, I went into seizure. I went into seizure back-to-back to back. In fact, I went into seizure six times after twenty-plus tequila shots, multiple grams of cocaine, and a pack of Sudafed. My body was dying. My heart was exploding, my chest was breaking, and my legs were rigid. Six times. For over an hour. Back-to-back. I still don't know how I crawled out of that room.

I do know I prayed to a God I left behind in the classrooms of Waverley College. I prayed to God that I did not want to leave my sons a legacy of a dead, loser, drug-addict father. With my last breaths, as I felt my body giving up and my heart stopping, I begged for another chance. I could feel a single tear on my cheek. The salty drop revived me. I was dead, but I had survived. I was given another chance.

Three days later, I went out and did it again. As I snorted another line in another inner Sydney toilet, I thought, "What the hell? Who gives a damn? I'm not scared of death." Crazy? You bet. The experience I went through, the near-death scare, the love of my sons, and the utter despair of me dying as a drug addict and alcoholic were not enough. I was gone. It was done. I was a walking two-line obituary and funeral card for my innocent sons.

When you know all hope is gone, and no one and nothing can save you, you give up and commit yourself to the end. It sounds dramatic, but it's not meant to be. It's a fact. Alcoholics and addicts in the final throes of active addiction are living refuse. Refuse gets thrown out. The very stuff that sustained us becomes our rubbish tip. We are born to die, but not this badly, and the sad single fact is that when addicts die, they take down all the unfortunate people hanging onto them. For me, when it seemed hopeless, it happened.

After another drama-filled and noisy failure of a night, I careened into my third rehab. I was sharing a room with two heroin addicts and a park drunk. We were all in withdrawal, none of us could sleep, and I was still hanging onto the thought that I was too good and too successful to be sharing a room in a psychiatric ward with a bunch of losers. Denial is a powerful friend and a dangerous enemy. It will ride with us into the gates of hell.

During the third night of no sleep, as I watched the park drunk from Newcastle strike out in the shadows to a ghost in his dreams, the metaphor of his sallow fist hit me like a lightbulb moment. I could not go any lower. This was my last chance. I had no more excuses. I was alone in rehab; ignored by my wife. My sons were shielded from me. My parents were in shock and utter pain at the shell their boy of so much promise had become. My beautiful sisters, Anne and Margie, could just smile at me, barely, and they held me like a brother they thought they may lose.

This was not a Hollywood movie or a reality TV show, where you build a room or dance a jig. This was life. Real life! Each city in the Western world is dotted with rehabs full of alcoholics, addicts, and anorexics just like me. Rehabs are the garbage bin of society. Like it or not, the need to succeed is also the seed to despair. It is the same impairment, just different strokes. Show me four bank CEOs, and I'll show you an addict or two.

Work obsession can be camouflaged by share prices and bank accounts. Camouflage tends to make the ugly pretty or the dangerous invisible. I can see through camouflage because I hid behind a number of dappled nets. Victories in this world are made by little people, and this little man made a little step. I decided I'd have a go at recovery. I gave in to what people call my disease. I put down my gun and took off my body armour. I stepped out from behind the nets. It was May 7, 1998, and I haven't had a drink of alcohol since that ugly night.

It's been over 23 years. I have made many mistakes since then, lost many things, hurt people, and used other forms of addiction just to get through days I thought would never end. Some days, I yell at the sky and rage against the very earth that sustains my life. I have met lawyers, bankers, and dentists who make the worst Kings Cross drug dealers look like playful puppies. Envy and greed can make the ugly pretty, and camouflage stuff. I have lapsed into depression, despair, and self-pity, but the legacy of that night and those three men is a legacy I cannot and will not forget.

I am the only man who walked out of that room into a future—out of the night and into the light. We had made promises to each other in that nuthouse camouflaged with Laura Ashley window drapes, that we would share birthdays and Happy New Year's celebrations. Sober. Together, we all chose life. But they fell deeper and are now fallen, and I got through. Those other three men tragically all succumbed to their addiction. I shared three treasured weeks of laughter, tears, and bad coffee with those brave and amazing men. They became my foot soldiers. They gave me a lightbulb moment which has been the catalyst for the dramatic change that has forged the rest of my life. And today my mission is to live life to the fullest. Giving and working with abundance whilst supporting with empathy, the vulnerable of this world and all those who are struggling with their mental health and battle addictions on a daily basis, so they too may find hope, love, acceptance and recovery.

adayintheweb@gmail.com

DAVE WILLIAMS

A GRIEVING PARTNER
FINDING HOPE AFTER A BRUSH WITH SUICIDE

"Standing over the kitchen bench with a chef's knife across my wrists, I knew I needed to make a decision. Either to stay as I was just existing, rather than living, or make the decision to change for the better."

Maybe you are like I was thinking – leave school, get a job and career, find a partner, have 2.4 kids and life would be pretty simple, right? As if life is on an uphill trajectory and in a straight line. Then, as you become more experienced you realise, life isn't like a straight line, it is more like a rollercoaster, with peaks and troughs all over the place. Let me share a bit of my story, let's teleport back to 2015.

Life was great, my training business was on course to be the most successful year ever, and my partner had found her love and was producing some amazing pictures. We had also been looking into the possibility of working with a couple of galleries to display her work. Great eh! But it doesn't end there.

If you'd have been with me on the December 10, 2015, you'd have been entering a white, square, clean smelling room that was quite cool and eerie. Covering about a third of the room was a blue shower type curtain.

As I pulled back the curtain, there she is. Helen, or Hel as I call her; my partner. Hel is about 5'10", with short brown hair and one of those grey streaks that run from the front to the back of her hair that she absolutely despises. Hel is full of fun, a real joker, the Jing to my Jang, my rock, my world, my sparring partner – Hel is the love of my life.

"Mr Williams, it is now time for you to leave." It was the voice I didn't want to hear of an officious looking Doctor in a three-quarter length white coat. You see, we were at the Royal

Derby Hospital, here in the UK, and Hel wasn't being prepared for an operation, she was being prepared for the morgue.

For the next couple of months things weren't too bad. I focused on Hel's family and indeed my own, But the fact was I was in denial and were using them to distract myself. I chose to put my head in the sand.

The reality was a bit different though as I was struggling to get out of bed on a daily basis and if I did, I was watching day-time TV. Well, when I say watching, reality was, the TV was on and I was staring at it but not absorbing any of it. When I was talking on the phone to friends and family, putting 'a brave face on' for the call to hopefully hide how I was feeling inside.

In essence I was just existing, and the fact was, I was at 'rock-bottom'. Not only had I lost the love of my life, but I had also lost my business. I wasn't functioning as a human being in my life personally nor in my business.

So, if you'd have been with me on this February evening in 2016, you'd have been sat on my corner black upholstery group, with white walls either side and a red feature wall in front of you. I know the TV is on the right-hand corner and the bookcase is in the left-hand corner of the room, but this particular evening, I couldn't see them as the darkness I was feeling inside was matching the darkness of this non-lit room. I was lost, lonely, depressed and wondering about the point of life.

Have you ever felt like that, lost and wondering the point of life?

I was listening to a lot of music that night which was very melancholic. Songs that resonated with me that Hel and I used to listen to, or other artists that I felt a real connection with. I just felt that I needed to have a connection to Hel and the better days we had. Because I was feeling so down, I hadn't eaten that day. I had lost confidence in myself and really couldn't see a future for myself. All our plans had evaporated like a Harry Potter spell. I was having constant thoughts of 'what is the point of going on'?

"I could always jump off the bridge at the bottom of the road, onto the main road, that would be pretty quick, I guess. And you hear of people drinking themselves to death, don't you? The problem is, I'm not keen on alcohol. I guess it would be easier with a knife then as no-one would find me for a while anyway."

I honestly, don't know what happened next as it is all a blur, it may have been seconds, or even minutes, I have no recollection at all. However, the next thing I knew, I was standing over the kitchen bench with a chef's knife across my wrists.

That was my 'lightbulb moment'. As I knew I needed to make a decision right then – either to stay as I was, just existing rather than living, realistically knowing I wouldn't be around much longer or make the decision to change for the better.

Deep down, I knew I needed help, but I'm a guy and guys don't ask for help do they? And if I had done the deed, whatever your beliefs about a greater force, I knew that Hel would have been so ashamed of me. Now, that is a powerful bit of leverage to change.

I went searching for answers to help me and tried a few things, but they didn't help me. So, I started putting some strategies in place and found they started to have an impact for me.

Now, as soon as you decide to change and take action, life becomes a bed of roses, right?

Not necessarily.

On many occasions, I thought I had turned the corner only to find another slide waiting to take me back a few steps. It seemed like my life was one big game of snakes and ladders, and I didn't have control of the dice.

Have you ever felt something similar, not feeling like you are in control?

Hel was my driver so I had to keep on going. I had to make her proud. 'What would Hel think of me'. She had left her impact on the people around her and it was my time to grab hold of that baton and continue with her legacy only in my name now.

So, I had to do much soul searching, and being totally honest, it was very uncomfortable at times, and being brutally transparent, I really struggled.

Visualise this – feeling rock bottom, emotionally numb, trying to excavate positive things about myself, my life and what I could do moving forward to get my life back on track. To stop existing in order to start living again. In fact, being honest, I felt I had failed.

But I knew this exercise needed to be done; it was something I MUST do. Therefore, I cheated! I put myself into what I imagined were Hel's shoes, and what she would say and do. You see, I was taking the emotional focus off myself and looking at the situation from a pretend third-party perspective. Imagine you are watching and enjoying a movie. You are watching that from a third-party perspective where you can see what is going on but cannot interact with it.

Eureka!

It worked for me and suddenly, I could start to see things in a different light and started making notes like crazy whilst I was in that frame of mind. Ok, I ended up scribbling most of them out, but it gave me a starting point. I printed out the summary of my goals and stuck them on my fridge so I could see them all the time.

Miraculously, my focus began to change, and I could start to look forward instead of backwards. The way I had been existing was trying to move forward staring in my rear-view mirror – the reality was, I crashed!

Because I was in such a bad frame of mind before my 'lightbulb moment', I had been talking to myself in a poorly way. It was very self-destructive and again, I hadn't realised it at the time. Here's the thing, I was using the most negative letter in the alphabet for nearly everything – 'T'. I was telling myself that I can'T do this, and I can'T do that. I have since summarised my 'can't' as 'Constantly Affirming Negative Talk!' Going through the afore mentioned exercise, I had that epiphany and realised what I had been doing. No wonder I had been struggling! I dropped the 'T' and started communicating to myself what I COULD do instead of telling myself what I couldn't do, turning can't into CAN!

As I was starting to feel better, I started doing more. Instead of struggling to get out of bed daily, listening to melancholy music, I began to emerge each day with more vigour and listening to more empowering music. For me it was rock music with a good beat. I also started exercising. It had been a while since I had done any exercise. Running was initially really slow and short distance. Little by little, this started to improve, just like everything else I had been doing; it was progress over perfection.

There were certain things that I was doing, but in the wrong way so I shifted my thoughts and actions and 'voila', things started to get better. I started sharing some of these strategies I had created with other people, and found they were getting great results in a shorter space of time too.

By chance, an email crossed my path to become a qualified coach. Hel and I had always been a magnet for others to come to and get their issues resolved and it seemed a good fit.

As I was about to leave for the course in London, I got a massive bout of anxiety and decided to cancel the course. My inner demons were saying, "Dave, how can you become a Master Coach when you can't even master yourself?"

Maybe you have experienced your 'inner demons' talking you out of things.

I gave myself a good talking to, being polite there, and rebooked the course as my drive was stronger than my 'inner demons'.

On entering the training room in a hotel by Heathrow Airport, I sat right at the front, just in front of the stage as I didn't want to miss a thing.

The trainers started their presentations and announced they were Tony Robbins (the world leader in life coaching) trainers. Just then a voice appeared in my head, not my 'inner demons' this time, but my 'inner angel'. In fact, it may have even been Hel, I don't know, "see Dave, you are in the right place."

So, where do you find me now? You find me as a #1 Bestselling Author, Award-Winning Master Coach and speaker who has had the pleasure of speaking in, and with clients in four countries around the world. Helping businesses increase their turnover, reduce staff turnover, and busy professionals and executives, overcome their challenges and start living life again instead of just existing. Even appearing on the same virtual stage as Tony Robbins and Dean Graziosi.

You see, now that I have had those experiences, I am better equipped to serve myself, and my clients at a greater level and life is great. I can now be more empathetic because of my experiences, although it was very painful at the time.

I now have a wonderful partner, and some very special people in my life who I have had the pleasure of meeting and have enriched my life beyond measure. I am so grateful to everyone who have been a part of my journey and have experienced some amazing things, and met some wonderful people, that I would never have considered possible, many years ago.

The wonderful thing about life now is that I get the privilege of being able to impact people and enhance their lives for the better. Which has resulted in impacting hundreds if not thousands around the world. That is not supposed to sound like hyperbole by any means. Indeed, I am interacting with you right now. You see, it is the ripple effect. Everyone is having an impact on the people they interact with. A bit like dropping a pebble in a pond and watching the ripples expand out from where the pebble was dropped. Here's the thing, those ripples can either be empowering or disempowering. The people I have worked with have turned their ripples into empowering ones, impacting others in their lives.

I can only share this story with you because of making the decision to change. Turning my situation from wanting to change to 'I MUST change'. Having my 'lightbulb moment' was the catalyst as I had to reach my pain threshold before I took that decision. If I hadn't had that moment, and made the right decision, you probably wouldn't be reading this, as no-one will have ever known my story as it would have stopped in 2016.

Has it been a journey with loads of peaks and troughs, 'hell yes', but it has helped me grow as a person and become a better person for it! In fact, it could be argued that "I have had more comebacks than Frank Sinatra!"

Now, obviously I don't know where you are on your journey, but as you have read my story, you will get hit by 'curve balls' along the way. If you are facing challenges currently, then my heart goes out to you but please note, that wherever you are, there is always 'light at the end of the tunnel'.

Will you make mistakes along the journey? Probably, as we are all human and that is how we learn. If you make a mistake, don't worry about it. Learn from it and make it better the next time. As Thomas Edison, inventor of the light bulb once said, "I have not failed. I just found 10,000 ways that won't work."

Always remember, you are a special, unique individual who has already achieved so many amazing things in life. You have the opportunity to take your life to a better level and have a phenomenal life, impacting others around you. The world needs you, your unique experiences, qualities, and outlook.

Wherever you are on your journey, "it is a chapter in your life and the beauty of it is 'you are in charge of the quill. If you don't like it, turn the page, and write another chapter.

If you have any comments about my story, then please let me know as it would be lovely to hear from you.

Thank you for reading and wishing you every success for the future.

Dave

dave@davewilliamscoaching.com

www.davewilliamscoaching.com

FERRY ZANDVLIET

2015 TERRORIST ATTACK SURVIVOR
A NEW PERSPECTIVE ON LIFE

"Walking the thin line between life and death, which is one of
people's greatest fears (including mine) has
made me a happier, more content, and perhaps
even a better person."

I can think of far more pleasant ways to experience a life changing lightbulb moment, but unfortunately for me, it was the moment I faced the horror of pure evil, a terrorist attack and stared death squarely in the face. The aftermath of that moment quickly rang out all over social media.

Twitter, Friday, November 13, 2015 1:30 AM: Paris attacks have come to an end. More than 120 casualties, most of whom were killed at the Bataclan. The police registered over 400 injured, many of them critically injured.

Earlier that night at *21:35, concert hall Le Bataclan, Paris* the band starts playing Kiss the Devil, one of their wildest songs. For the first time, a little mosh pit forms in front of the stage. The crowd loses it and turns into a swarming mass of people running around and pushing into each other in a rough, yet also friendly way. My mate Frank's beer gets knocked out of his hands. Bob, Dexter, and Frank enter the mosh pit. I stay put; I'm afraid to do those kinds of things now because of my weak ankle. I can see people going wild and enjoy watching the mayhem from a safe distance.

I was once at a Limp Bizkit concert where the lead singer made everyone in the crowd crouch down low to then all jump up together again. This must be what is going on here was what I thought. EODM isn't a very serious band, they can be kind of silly. Maybe this is some kind of a stupid joke that I'm not getting.

First, I fall down forward kind of diagonally, and my hands just about manage to break my fall. They're resting on the backs of several other people that have also all fallen over forward. I then turn over to lie on my back, which is hard because my feet are entangled. I see many others around me do the same thing. I'm lying on top of an enormous pile of people, there must be about five people underneath me. I feel very exposed this high up—right at the top, there's nowhere for me to go. My feet are stuck under the shoulders of the person in front of me, but apart from that my hands and upper body are free to move. Instead of facing the stage, I'm now facing the entrance. I'm lying left from the stage. The edge is about 10 feet away from me. Everyone around me is completely tangled up.

I look over at the entrance to the hall and see a few men standing there, and I know they aren't security guards. They're about thirty feet away from me. I can see one of them very well. He's holding a gun. He's pointing the barrel up at the ceiling - he's reloading. He's wearing all black clothes and his chest shows that there's something underneath his clothes. A bulletproof vest perhaps?

I'm not sure what's going on but I do know that my life is in danger, just like everyone else in the crowd. Nobody utters a sound. A deadly silence reigns.

THE ATTACK

21:40PM - I hear the words, "Allah Akbar" resound through the venue. "God is great" and I am sprawled out in the most vulnerable of positions, face-up, on top of a huge pile of people. I have no idea how many. How long have I been lying here? Is it one minute? One hour? I have no idea. Time seems to be standing still. It's dead quiet. The only sound I hear is the heavy breathing of the people that are lying underneath me in a tangled mess. You can hear the fear of death. You can feel it too. This is real. So, there I am, lying on the floor, with all my savings in the bank, all of my pent-up anger, and all of my fears.

Why have I always focused on work so much? Why am I always angry at everything and everyone? Why am I always such a pain in the ass? Why am I messing around again with this half-assed commitment to my current relationship? None of that matters any more. My life is going to end in a minute. My brain is telling me so, it's as if it's saying - it's okay, stay calm, just lie there, it'll all be over soon. I never thought my life would end this way.

Even though I am lying here in this theatre with over a thousand other people, I feel so lonely and alone. So, this is the place where my life's going to end. In silence, on the floor of a concert hall, in Paris, of all places. I hadn't even been in this city for twenty years until today. Turns out it's not a cliché: when you think you're about to die, your life flashes by in front of you. I can see an ocean, a beautiful wave, a beach with perfect, white sand. Mexico, I think, Playa del Carmen. The most beautiful beach I've ever seen in my life. In one of the waves, I can see myself: as a baby, toddler, teenager, adult, and then suddenly back here in Paris. It's almost as if your brain wants to show you everything again briefly. For the very last time. The bullet is coming for me. I'm one hundred per cent sure about that. Three Kalashnikovs are pointed at me. I close my eyes and wait for everything to go black.

Wednesday, August 21, 2019, UN Offices, Vienna

Why on Earth did I agree to do this? I'm breaking out in a cold sweat. My heart is beating in my throat and I'm a total ball of nerves. I'm sitting in a large conference hall at the United Nations Offices in Austria. I'm looking out over a bunch of tables arranged in a U-shape seating all sorts of international guests that all have a little name plate in front of them. Next to their name, it says which country they're from. Qatar, Japan, Kazakhstan, Belgium, the United States, and so on. The table I'm sitting at isn't part of the U-shape, it's right in the middle of the open space at the top of the U. This is because I'm sitting at the speaker's table and I'm about to deliver a speech.

Just let that sink in for a minute: I HAVE TO DELIVER A SPEECH TO THE UNITED NATIONS! Me, who never had the courage to speak in front of a group of people about to give a lecture in English to a pretty intimidating group of people. At least, that's what it feels like. I'm literally the only one in the room that's not wearing a suit. The atmosphere is highly charged and I haven't seen anyone smile so far.

This is the umpteenth step I've taken outside of my comfort zone. Because, guess what? Turns out I'm actually good at speaking to large groups of people. The thing that used to scare me to death has become my full-time job. Sometimes I can hardly believe it myself. It all happened so incredibly quickly. Sometimes I can hardly believe it's all happening.

As a speaker, I go to places that I had never believed I would go to for work: Las Vegas, San Diego, New York City, San Francisco, Los Angeles, Palm Springs, and to top it all off: Honolulu in Hawaii. And the rollercoaster just keeps thundering on, because today I'm here in beautiful Vienna. Although, I have to say that the place where I'm giving my lecture at the UN is very grey and industrial. But, here I am.

I got asked to do this only a week ago via a message that came through on LinkedIn:

Dear Ferry, thank you for accepting my LinkedIn request. Would you allow me to be direct and ask you a question? As you might have seen from my LinkedIn profile, my team and I work on all sorts of types of radicalization, extremism, and polarization. Our international partners have asked us if we could put someone from Europe forward as a speaker for an international commemorative gathering about terrorist attack survivors and victims. The organization is the United Nations and this meeting is going to take place on August 21, in Vienna.

I can imagine this request is a little bit last minute, but I wanted to put you forward.

Looking forward to your reply, Najib

My first reaction was 'I'm scared witless! But I'm definitely going. Hell yeah!' The timing is a little inconvenient though. I've just spent a whole weekend at Lowlands, one of the largest music festivals in the Netherlands. A true Valhalla for me. Since 2001, I've been to the festival the entire weekend almost every year. I've seen nearly all of my favourite artists play there: Queens of the Stone Age, System of a Down, Iggy Pop, Mark Lanegan, and TOOL. I would never have even dreamed of the possibility of being part of this festival's line-up. Yes. I can still hardly believe it, that I Ferry Zandvliet, spoke at Lowlands in 2018. I was invited to give a short speech. One of the many surreal experiences that I've had since that awful night in 2015.

For today's presentation in Vienna, I came back from my favourite festival a day earlier. I wanted to prepare properly. The organization told me I only had twelve minutes to speak. That's so hard for me. Nowadays, I can easily talk for an hour non-stop, but such a short slot is just way more difficult. You can't improvise, every sentence has to be spot-on. I'm the last speaker today. I've been feeling like I'm dying for the last forty minutes while listening to all the men in their suits. Whatever they say completely goes over my head. This is a new type of nervousness that I haven't experienced in my career as a speaker yet.

When the time finally came and they introduced me, I forgot to take my notes to the desk where I had to speak. Despite this, I manage to talk fairly smoothly for the entire twelve minutes. I told them in great detail about the attack, the media chaos, the disappointing lack of support we received when we came back to the Netherlands, the immense suffering I went through as a result of PTSD, meeting the father of one of the terrorists, and how the attack has made me a happier person. An enormous round of applause followed and this became another experience to cross off of my bucket list. A list that's getting shorter and shorter.

When I got back to my hotel, I read the following tweet on the official United Nations Twitter account: *"It's you who decides whether you are a victim or a survivor." Ferry Zandvliet on rejecting hate & forming a friendship with the father of the terrorist who tried to kill him. He is sharing the truth of his experience which helps to aid healing and advance understanding.*

How did I make it this far? How has that horrendous night in 2015 manage to enrich my life so greatly? How has the Bataclan attack got rid of that angry little guy inside myself and made me happier? Yes, you read that correctly. Walking the thin line between life and death, which is one of people's greatest fears (including mine) has made me a happier, more content, and perhaps even a better person.

How? Sometimes I'm not even sure anymore, but I'll try to explain it.

THE MORNING OF 2015

It's a beautiful autumn day, there's not a cloud in the sky and the sun is beating down. Yesterday was an amazing day. I signed a contract with a new physiotherapist. Combining the bar work and physiotherapy is unsustainable. The clashing schedules are doing me in pouring beer until late at night and then trying to do serious work with patients the next morning. I feel like I'm sabotaging my body. So, this contract is the solution to my problems.

I had a sense that things needed to change. I was feeling exhausted and deep down I knew I wouldn't be able to go on living like this - burning the candle at both ends for much longer. Why did it have to take such a tragic event to open my eyes to finally be able to see the beauty and awe of life in such simple ways?

Since that night, I now often get asked: "Are you still not done with that Paris-story?" I can tell you I'm done with that horrific bloody part of my story; I don't like the many requests to always talk about it. But, there is now so much more to this story and all the positivity that has come my way out of something that was so horrendous. It has reshaped and repurposed my life in a way I never thought possible, and I will talk about that until the day I die.

I still have so many thoughts and emotions swirling around in my mind about that night.

I think about the terrorists, those bastards that have completely messed up my life.

I see myself crawling across the floor and over other people in the Bataclan Theatre, in full-on survival mode.

I think about the phone conversation with my mother while I'm running down the alley, I relive the panic in her voice.

I think about the relief that I felt when I found out Bob was still alive.

I think about the love that I then felt at home with those total strangers. My new family.

I feel my eyes well up when I think back to the moment that Lionel got down on the other sofa with a blanket to keep an eye on me. Such a beautiful gesture. Isn't it bizarre, that within a space of four hours, you get to see both the worst and best of humanity?

The surreal feeling of being in the middle of a world news story.

Being reunited with my family, friends, and co-workers.

The tsunami of WhatsApp messages from people I know and people I don't know.

And just for a moment I catch myself lost in my thoughts as I whisper to myself 'how cool was that. I've been on live TV three times now to share my story of survival'.

For a fleeting moment, a smile appears on my face when I think about all this. Not because there is anything to smile about at all, but because it's so surreal. And then I quickly realise through a pleather of emotions, when I lay my head on my pillow later tonight, and I wake up in the morning tomorrow, it's not going to be a normal day ever again. One, where I can just jump into the shower, pack my bag, and head for the clinic. I know that's not going to happen. I'm still in that Tarantino horror movie.

That same sentence comes to my mind over and over again, What the f*** is all of this going to do to me? What's in store for me from here on? And then I ask myself? If the Ferry from the future would be able to talk to me right now, what would I say to myself? Then the ultimate lightbulb moment realisation comes: "Stay calm my boy, the years to come are going to be very tough. Your parents' divorce will pale in comparison to what's in store for you. You're going to go through hell, and that hell will last a long time. But you'll make it out. Seriously, you have no idea how this is going to enrich your life in the years to come. Dreams will come true. You're capable of much more than you think right now or ever believed was possible. You're going to change lives. Inspire people. You're going to travel the world with your story. That Ferry that always plays the victim card, that's always angry and often refuses to take charge of his own life, that Ferry is going to disappear completely. You're going to become the best version of yourself, and you're going to do it all yourself. Hang in there…

The night my life flashed before my eyes, the lightbulb moment that hit me right between the eyes, has led me to share my story of survival and hope and how I found the true meaning of life with audiences all around the world. At one very special talk, I share the following:

TED Talk Schiedam, March 30, 2017

Standing backstage at the Theatre aan de Schie in the Dutch city of Schiedam, I take a peek at an immense stage which I have to enter in a minute. From where I'm standing, backstage on the right, I can just catch a glimpse of the gigantic auditorium, which is almost completely full. In the last few months, I've given a few lectures to the police force and at schools. But those were always groups of thirty to forty people. In Schiedam, here today, there are almost 600 people in the audience. The host is sharing something about the background of my talk with the audience. I can't hear exactly what he's saying but I'm waiting for the moment he says my name to take the stage. It feels surreal to have to step onto that stage soon. I can feel my pupils dilate to the max and my hands are dripping in sweat. I wipe them off on my jeans for the millionth time. Why did I say yes to doing this? What if I forget my lines? What if they don't laugh at my jokes? What if…?

My thoughts are all over the place. It's as if my instinct wants to protect me from a big mistake and screams that I shouldn't go ahead with this. The host says my name and I walk onto the stage anyway. I'm about to give a TED Talk. TED is an acronym for Technology, Entertainment, and Design. A format from California where the idea is for the speakers to explain an idea, experience, or expertise about a certain topic using straightforward language in a maximum of eighteen minutes. I've been a big fan of the platform for years, and I didn't hesitate for a second when I was asked to participate. The preparation process consisted of two rounds of auditions and coaching. But after my first audition, the jury gave their unanimous verdict, "Don't change anything about it." That was about four months ago, and I haven't sat still since. To prepare as best as I can, I've offered to give talks at police departments and high schools. Because, you know, standing on stage in front of a crowd giving a speech isn't something I'm a natural at.

With my shoulders slightly drooping, I step onto the stage and walk toward a red circle on the floor where I must stand during my entire talk. Several cameras are recording at the same time in order to register today's entire presentation. As I'm walking toward the circle, I can feel my hands get even sweatier and my eyes get even bigger. I look at some people sitting in the first two rows. One lady winks at me as if to say, "You can do it, kid." For some reason I can't bring myself to look past the first two rows. I know at least twenty rows of people are sitting behind the first two, but I'm too scared to lift my gaze much more. When I get to the red circle and stop, I take a deep breath and start my talk.

"I'd like to tell you about a very special time in my life, the time when I survived a terrorist attack along with the guys you can see behind me. This photo was taken just before the Eagles of Death Metal concert in Paris, at the end of 2015. You can see we were really looking forward to it. It was a fun night. The next photo is shocking, it was taken after the IS terrorist had opened fire and shot ninety people to death, injuring another three hundred."

You could hear a pin drop in the theatre. Six-hundred people are looking at me with bated breath as I take them on a journey through my story. I tell them how the party turned into a warzone that night. The reptilian response from everyone at the club, how I pretended I was dead, and wanted to hide behind someone for the shower of bullets. About the terrorists I saw standing in front of the entrance of the club. About my mind that quickly projected all of my memories as I was lying there waiting for a bullet to hit me. About my escape route to get out and how I was helplessly running through the streets of Paris after and how I met and was taken in by a very kind woman Veronique who took me in just moments after the attack and how her kindness, the kindness of a perfect stranger in my greatest time of need, mellowed me and changed my life. About how ecstatically happy I was when I heard my close friend Bob was still alive.

I also shared some of the key life learnings that have emerged out of my life since that night - letting go of anger. Just try it. Even if it's just for a short time and take a good look at what happens around you when you do. It's so easy. Also, choose a person you know to tell them what he or she means to you. And this should be someone that has never heard this from you before. It's so easy and so incredibly valuable. These are the things that have enriched my life so much over the last few years. Seriously. I could never have imagined I would talk about that bloodbath, that nightmare that I went through and say, "I wouldn't have missed it for the world. Thank you."

As I finish sharing my story in this auditorium an enormous applause ensues. A standing ovation, even. I don't know what's happening to me. Six hundred people are standing up and clapping for me. I feel my sweaty hands drying up, my eyes getting smaller and a gigantic weight falling off my shoulders. It's impossible to suppress my massive smile. As proud as a peacock I take a bow. I rejoice in my moment, even though it feels strange. Now that everyone's standing up, the auditorium looks even bigger. Suddenly I can see the rows in the back and the balconies. In many ways, my talk today lacks nuance on many levels. I talk about anger and fear as if they're things you can simply let go of, but of course it's a lot more complex than that. And I say I never would have wanted to miss it. Of course, you can't say that about a terrorist attack. Even so, today here in Schiedam, a seed has been sown. A seed that needs to do a lot of growing, but it's a start. And it's the start of something I want to do a heck of a lot more of.

www.ferryzandvliet.nl

JOHN KILLICK

**AUSTRALIA'S GREATEST ESCAPE ARTIST
LIVING BEYOND REGRET – THE EX-BANK
ROBBER GIVING BACK**

"A chill ran through me, and I froze. How could I have done it?
Not once but many times. I knew I couldn't change my past, but
I could change what I did with my future."

When you reach my age, you often look back and think about the way it could have been. In retrospect the mistakes you made when you were young often seem not just irresponsible, but prime examples of stupidity.

If only I'd had a mentor. But, on the contrary I came from a dysfunctional family where Dad was always drunk on Friday and Saturday nights. When he was drunk he was violent. An ex-champion boxer who still loved to fight and terrorise the neighbours - and us. Us being my mother and adopted younger brother. I was also adopted and had no idea who my paternal parents were.

Sometimes we would sleep under the house to avoid his violent rages. Sometimes in the middle of winter it would be too cold to sleep under the house and we would walk the streets until dad fell into an inebriated sleep and we could creep back into the house and our beds. I missed a lot of schooling. I retreated into a world of fantasy via books, comics, and radio serials.

I was a good kid. I didn't steal or break the law. Despite my dysfunctional background I was destined to be a law-abiding citizen.

Then one cold Sunday night in late June in 1959 my mother fell out of bed after taking an overdose of sleeping tablets. She was seriously ill. Jumping on my bike I rode to a phone booth and rang our local doctor. But we owed him money for those sleeping tablets so he wouldn't come. That delay cost my mother

her life. By the time we got her to hospital in an ambulance it was too late.

My mother, a good woman, in every sense of the word, was dead. That day I packed my bag and left. My father couldn't believe it. He pleaded with me to stay. But I couldn't. I blamed him for my mother's death.

I had enough money to book into a cheap boarding house in Burwood. I had to share the room with a guy who was about thirty years old. His name was Joe. He was a big strong guy who loved to wrestle. When he tried to wrestle with me, making sexual overtures at the same time, I cried foul. Although he apologised, the damage was done.

The shock of my mother's death, leaving the family home and the attempted sexual assault by a stranger all within twenty-four hours impacted heavily on me. I was alone in the world. I had no job, no home, no money and no family or friends who I could turn to.

THIS was my first light bulb moment.

Not in a good way, but in a perverse rebellious way. From this day I decided that in order for me to survive, it would be me against the world. Rules and laws didn't matter anymore. My mother always obeyed the law and played by the rules. Look what it had got her.

My first crime involved Joe the wrestler. He told me he was ripping off the government by claiming unemployment benefits under different names. Stealing one of his bank books I booked into a different rooming house and practised his signature until I was satisfied it would pass muster. I withdrew a sum of money from it and nervously left the bank. Technically it was my first bank robbery.

But the nosey lady in charge of the rooming house saw the discarded withdrawal slips in the bin and called the police. I was arrested and spent the night at Albion Street Boy's Shelter. Surprisingly my father arrived the next day and bailed me out.

Too little too late.

Although he tried to redeem our relationship it was impossible. I was now a different person to the boy he had known a few weeks earlier. I again walked out of the house, this time to never return.

I teamed up with a few boys older than me and began to live a full-on life of crime from shoplifting to smash and grabs to being rolling drunks. For meals we would eat in cafes and restaurants then run off without paying.

We soon graduated to break and enters. That didn't last long. One day me and two accomplices tried to pawn some clothes from a break and enter. Being a suspicious man by nature the pawnbroker called the police when he noticed the clothing was for a much bigger man. Not wanting to go to prison on his own one of them who I'd thought was a mate gave us up to the authorities. Appreciating his cooperation, the authorities let him go and sent the other two of us to Long Bay. I was still only seventeen and legally should not have been there.

In January 1960 Long Bay Penitentiary as it was then, was an extremely tough institution. Bashings by prisoners and guards was a common thing. Good looking boys were much sought after as cell mates not necessarily for their conversational skills. Some young guys were even sexually assaulted in the showers.

The cells had no sanitation - a bucket with disinfectant sufficed as a toilet for three men; a rusty jug of water was the drinking water, no sheets or pyjamas and no radio or television. Books were rare, usually paperback westerns were the best I could get. Lights off at nine pm. No phone calls and a fortnightly visit of twenty minutes was allowed while your visitor stood behind wire mesh with a guard standing there listening to everything you had to say.

You could write a one page letter per week which would first be read by a guard who would cross out any objectionable material.

During my first week there I was attacked by a young German when I had the audacity to beat him in a game of chess; I managed to get the better of him while everyone watched. Somehow after that I survived three months without any more serious drama.

In April 1960 I was released on a bond. You would think that these experiences would have influenced me to take the straight and narrow. Instead, it made me realise that petty criminals committed petty crimes. If I was going to be a criminal I would be one of the best. And in the sixties, bank robbers and safe breakers were the elite criminals - at least to other criminals. To the police they were menaces who had to be stopped at all costs. And, to the movie makers, bank robbers were the best.

When I decided to become a bank robber, I was surprised to learn that in Australia bank robberies were rare. The four most infamous bank robbers were in prison: Darcy Dugan bank robber/escapee serving life; Kevin Simmons bank robber/ escapee serving life; Peter Walker and Ronald Ryan both bank robber/escapees just recaptured. Ryan would be hanged, and Walker would get thirty-six years.

Not great incentives there to rob banks. Plus, some of the bank tellers had guns. Nevertheless, as the infamous American bank robber Willy Sutton said, "That's where the money is."

In late January 1966, I robbed my first bank and took the manager's pistol.

On 14 February, 1966, - the day Australia turned to decimal currency - I became Australia's first C Day bandit when I robbed a bank in Cabramatta. I then travelled to Melbourne and robbed a bank in Kensington − this time armed tellers came after me and fired shots at me. Not long afterwards I was arrested at a dance studio while I was learning to tango.

Sent to the notorious Pentridge Prison, I made a couple of serious escape attempts - as all good bank robbers do - and was sent to the hell-hole H Division where I was bashed and humiliated and forced to break rocks most of the day.

Ronald Ryan was waiting to be hanged while I was there. When he was hanged on February 3, 1967, the gaol was like a powder keg with the prisoners ready to riot. The execution was so controversial that it became the last one in Australia.

Just before I was released from Pentridge in September 1972, I testified at the Royal Commission that there was no place like H Division to illustrate man's Inhumanity to Man and the media acknowledged this.

And H Division only hardened me further.

My attitude of 'me against the world' was now set in concrete.

Since that time, I have been convicted of bank robberies in South Australia, New South Wales, and Queensland. I escaped from prison guards at gunpoint during a trip to hospital in Brisbane and in March 1999, I escaped in a helicopter from Silverwater maximum security after my girlfriend forced the pilot to land on the oval at gunpoint.

At that stage, I had become number One on Australia's Most Wanted. I had done what I set out to do way back in the early sixties.

I had become a notorious bank robber escapee just like Darcy Dugan and the others.

But at what cost?

Over thirty years in prison.

But it is more than that.

What damage had I done to others?

I always figured I wasn't hurting anyone when I robbed banks. I hated banks. They foreclosed on our house when I was a child. Forced us to live in a dilapidated rundown house where my mother became depressed and eventually took her life. Banks were bad. I never shot anyone or hurt anyone.

That was my attitude until about five years ago when I had the **great lightbulb moment.** I went into a city bank to deposit some money. I was the only customer.

The young female teller was immaculately groomed, friendly, and attractive. It flashed through my mind that there was a time when I might have pointed a loaded weapon at this young woman and threatened her in the process of robbing the bank.

A chill ran through me**, and I froze**.

How could I have done it? Not once but many times.

I tried to imagine how this girl would feel — the fear, the horror — and later, the trauma.

I felt ashamed. No doubt I had terrorised people just like her. Somebody's daughter, somebody's wife or their mother.

My justification? It had been me against the banks.

I finally realised in this moment, all these years my thinking had been so distorted. Wrong Killick! It had been you with a loaded weapon against unarmed, innocent people.

The young teller handed me my receipt, and with a beautiful smile, said, "Thank you, John."

Did she know who I was?

No. She had simply noticed my name on the statement.

"A pleasure," I said, meaning it.

This was my greatest lightbulb moment as I suddenly had a revelation of the gravity of my actions and how wrong they had been in the past.

It felt so great that day to be able to walk rather than run out of that bank. I had deep regrets. Even though I was a changed man, I knew I couldn't go back and change the past but what I did realise in that moment, was that I had the capacity to give back in the future in the years I had left.

During all those years in prison I had never used an email nor social media. I heard guys talking about missing their Facebook accounts when they returned to gaol. Although I was seventy-two when I was released I was determined to learn about these things. I got on Facebook and made friends with many people including some from overseas.

I emailed lots of publishers about a book I was writing, and I began to learn the ropes. Soon I realised the abject poverty many people who were my friends, especially in the Philippines were living under and I wanted to make a difference. There were no government pensions for these poor people. A mobile phone and Facebook were the only opportunities they had to gain a sponsor.

In 2015 I began to sponsor a girl and still do to this day. She is now married with a beautiful baby. They are still struggling but surviving. After eventually achieving my goal of publishing some books, I was able to afford to help a few of her family members also and a girl in Africa. Then I went on to sponsor some beautiful children who really needed support in Kyrgyzstan. Their father had walked out leaving their mother to be the sole supporter. My beautiful ex-wife flew over and spent two months there helping this family when the mother became sick. It cost us $10,000. I did these things without wondering if we could afford it. I just knew that these people needed it more than we did.

The joy I get from seeing these beautiful people, mainly children being able to learn at school, wear decent clothes and eat decent food is better than any joy I ever received from gambling even when I won. What I do is only a drop in the bucket. But fifty dollars in the Philippines can feed an entire family for a week. I do what I can today, because I can. I know within myself that I am giving back. It's a very different life compared to the past where I just used to take.

I can never undo the wrongs I have done, but I can still do a lot of good things. That is what I try to do. And I feel much better about myself because I know it comes from a heart that is genuine. I know what it's like to be a young boy on the streets not knowing how I would survive. Afterall, that is where this whole story started. And now it's come full circle, I have finally found my purpose after so many years and much suffering to give out of the love in my heart for these the people that I care about so much.

johnrkillick@gmail.com

JORGE VALDES

LIVING A LIFE OF REDEMPTION
THE FORMER COLOMBIAN CARTEL DRUG BOSS
REWRITING HIS STORY

"That was the moment when I thought, 'I AM DONE. TODAY MY LIFE WILL CHANGE'. I Didn't know what change would mean but all I knew was that I wanted out of that life. That I needed to change."

I never set out to become one of the founding members of Colombia's biggest drug cartel or to end up in a tell all on the big screen Netflix series, 'Cocaine Cowboys, The Kings of Miami'. That was a life I am not proud of. As a young kid all I ever wanted was to make my parents proud and to become self-sufficient. But I got sucked into the pseudo-American dream. The one where society and media tell you you're only successful when you have earned millions of dollars and have the lifestyle everyone else only ever dreams of. Then you would really be somebody.

I had grown up in the midst of extreme poverty and watched my parents struggle immensely. This wasn't the life I wanted for myself or for them. I had big plans. I started out just like every other young guy sets out, having dreams and goals in life to be financially stable and make it on my own. In fact, I was the least likely person to ever become a drug dealer - I was a nerd. During the day I worked full time for the Federal Reserve Bank and studied full time at night. I drew lines and had a clear vision about how my life would be. I would Graduate from the university of Miami in accounting, save hard and earn enough money to go to Law School and then become a millionaire by thirty. But, I found a shortcut.

After I finished at the university my accounting professor asked me to come and work for him. The first job he gave me to do was the books for a local grocery store. Unbeknownst to me, I soon realized they were drug dealers.

At first it seemed innocent. I wasn't officially doing anything wrong, right? I was just doing my job and I could look the other way, but then when the dollars started being splashed before me like giant glittering diamonds, enticing me and pulling me in, greed took hold and I crossed the line. A line I never thought I would cross. Within months, millions of dollars were flooding in and with it came this kind of lifestyle that every kid in the world wanted. Finally, I was someone. I never in a million years imagined that this would become the life I would live.

I was twenty-one years old, had millions of dollars, houses, private jets, fast and expensive cars; was dating beautiful women. I had more money than I knew what to do with. You would think I would be the happiest guy in the world right? Wrong. I may have had everything, but Joy and happiness was not there. The happiness was fleeting and only lasted a short time. No amount of earthly treasure could fill the void inside and instead I kept searching for the new high. I kept dodging, rolling, flipping high dices, but for how long? Eventually my addiction to fame, success, money, and sex, took me right into the belly of hell. Ironically, in the world's eyes I had it all, yet all I wanted was to die.

My first wife was a beauty queen, and my second wife was beautiful and young, but it meant nothing to me. Both those marriages lasted less than three years between them. I thought when I dated beautiful women I was going to be happy. But I was miserable. The truth is if we don't find joy within ourselves, with ourselves, nothing will ever make us happy. I had a sex addiction, and it was out of control.

In fact, I was hoping I would get killed. I thought my happiness would be my next super car. I had millions of dollars in exotic cars and yet I was miserable. Every night we lay down in bed and then when we awake and look in the mirror we must ask ourselves if we like what we see? When I realized I didn't like what I saw, even though I had death threats every day, someone saying they were going to kill me, I didn't care, in fact, looking back, I welcomed death. I had reached the zenith, the pinnacle of what I thought would bring me joy, happiness and in fact it did neither, it meant absolutely nothing.

One fateful day in April of 1979, flying for a meeting with a prominent person in Nicaragua, our plane went down over the jungles of Panama. There I was arrested and tortured for twenty-eight days. I thought I would rather die in that foreign prison than to cooperate and tell on the Cartel. Escaping barely with my life and left with injuries so bad, that for the following five years every time I went to the toilet, I would pee blood. I was sent to the United States and charged with heading the largest drug conspiracy in the history of America, given two million dollars bail and when I went to trial and was found guilty, I was sentenced to fifteen years in a federal prison.

In prison, because I had more money and power than all the other inmates, I still lived a lavish lifestyle even though behind bars. While in there I married my second wife. I ended up serving five of the fifteen years and after my release went straight back into the same lifestyle. I was hateful and wanted revenge for what I thought had been done to me; yet this time things were different, and I now realized that what I had once believed was a victimless crime (drug importation) was actually killing children. In 1986 the world totally changed for me when my baby girl Krystle had come into the world and soon to be followed by two more beautiful children. But even though I now had newfound responsibilities, that didn't stop my out of control sex addiction from sabotaging that which should have been everything to me and I ended up cheating on my second wife and lost my family; not seeing my children every day destroyed me, this is not who I truly was.

I was desperate and I wanted to change, I wanted out. I remember one day when I asked a good friend, "how did you quit?" He said to me, "it's like being pregnant. You're either pregnant or you're not. You have to change your life and change your surroundings." I made the phone call and walked away from the cartel, knowing that it would almost definitely mean I would be killed within the next month or two.

I wanted so much to be different. I wanted desperately to be the person my dear parents had raised with tremendous principles and integrity. Not the scum of the earth drug dealer I had become. Even though I walked away from that life in the cartel, I still had loads of money and thought I could live out an exciting life as a millionaire playboy. But, the feds who had been tracking my every move and tracing my every cent had other plans. They were watching me and before long they would pounce bringing my house of cards down like dominos and cascading my new life into the abyss.

But before they did, I had moved into a multimillion dollar ranch with the intention to legitimately make money the honest way, breeding quarter horses. It was at this ranch one fateful day that an incident changed my life forever. This was a pivotal moment that shook me to my core. This was my lightbulb moment.

My ex-wife had dropped off my little girl - the love of my life, one afternoon to my ranch where I was partying with beautiful movie stars. I told my bodyguard to take her to the nanny and keep her in her room and not let her out until the morning when we would have breakfast, and I went back to my party. My little girl got out of her room and all of a sudden, I heard her knocking on my bedroom door! She was calling out, "daddy, daddy, it's me." I froze and started to shiver. I realized in that very moment, here is the only thing that is sacred and holy in my life, the only thing I care about in the world, my most sacred possession, and I can't let her in. I instantly felt broken. It's almost like you are on a boat and your child is in the water drowning and you are touching their fingertips, but you can't hold onto them.

I told the women to leave out the window and I went into the shower and tried to wash all the filth of me, and I couldn't. I let an hour pass and I went out of my bedroom to get a glass of water thinking Krystle had gone back to bed, and to my despair when I opened the door, there she was outside lying on the floor crying. That was the moment when I thought, 'I am done Today my life will change.' I didn't know what change would mean but all I knew was that I wanted out of that life. That I needed to change.

In the bible, it says - out of the mouth of children, I will speak. I believe out of the mouth of my baby girl. I was being sent a very loud message even though I was a hard core atheist at the time. I believed in myself and nobody else. But what I did know was this. Who I had become, was not who I inherently was. I knew I needed to change. I did not know what that meant but I knew one thing, if I was going south I would go north, if I was going east I would go west, I simply needed to totally change my life.

The first thing I did was to leave my environment. I realized that if the friends you have, help you participate in the life that leads you to death, they are not your friends. It's ironic that thousands of people said they would die for me, yet when I went to prison for ten years, not a single friend remained. They looked like Olympic runners. The only people that remained and were there for me, were my mum, dad and my brother JC, who I had abandoned, yet he never turned his back on me.

I knew that I couldn't go back. Back is only going to lead me to destruction. I had ended up destroying all the relationships around me and I destroyed myself in the process. I knew I had to go forward. I knew I was created to be a lot better than that - we are not defined by our past. There is hope. There is redemption. Rock bottom is so hard to explain. Everyone who has been there knows it. In prison I would come to believe that there is a God who loves us and forgives us but the consequence of our choices is always going to be there.

Ironically, just prior to my miracle, I had hired a karate instructor to teach me karate. There was something so different about this guy. He lived a humble life and in my opinion at the time I thought, an inferior life. He had an old car, old house and was married to the same woman for twenty-five years. Yet he was so happy and constantly filled with Joy. I wanted what he had. He told me he was a Christian, but what was most intriguing was that he said he had an intimate relationship with Jesus; I could not understand that as I was surrounded by many people and I did not have an intimate with anyone; what was he talking about? Three years later when my divorce was final and I saw my ex-wife drag my little girl away, I was so desperate that even though I was an atheist I knew I had to give his Jesus ago. I didn't even know if he was real or not, but I had absolutely nothing left to lose, I had tried everything else.

Three months later, after leaving the cartel for almost four years, the feds finally got me, and it came to be that I was arrested for the second time. This time once and for all, I wanted to put things right. I forfeited all my millions and pleaded guilty without knowing if I would be jailed for life or not. I was tired of fighting and if this Jesus was going to change my life I just knew I had to come clean and start my life all over again despite the consequences. But one thing I did have this time was peace.

I spent almost five years in prison and in that time was focused not on the past, but my future and how I could change my life and rebuild it. There I became celibate and remained that way for seven years until I married the true love of my life. This time my third wife would be a true blessing from heaven.

After being with porn stars and so many women over the years, it would take a miracle to be satisfied with just one woman; my mind had been so corrupted over the years, yet I prayed that I could love her, and be satisfied having sex with just one woman. And that is exactly what happened. I eventually found a woman I adored so much not for who she was on the outside but for who she was on the inside, and I have been married to this one beautiful woman now for 25 years. My wife now is the love of my life. Every day I am more in love with my wife and my life than ever. We have an amazing relationship with two children together and four children from previous relationships; I am who I am today because I waited until God sent the woman He had created just for me. I truly believe this.

When I surrendered to follow Jesus, my life, at first, went from bad to horrific, yet I couldn't go back to my old life.

Redemption for me was a long process. It is a process that when things do not go as you believe they should go - when life keeps throwing challenges and obstacles at you, you keep reminding yourself to keep moving forward telling yourself that you simply cannot go back, there is nothing but destruction and chaos in the past. I know this was my process, this was my thinking. I simply took one little step at a time and eventually things started to change. I started to find meaning and joy.

Whilst in prison I wanted to know all I could about this Jesus I had surrendered to, and I began to study Theology. I earned a Bachelor's degree, then I started my Master's degree. When I got out I finished my Master's degree followed by a PhD from Loyola University In Chicago. When I finished my PhD my father passed away; he was my best friend in the whole world and I was missing him terribly, then suddenly It hit me, my father had not given me anything materially, he had nothing to give, yet he gave me the greatest gift a father can give his child - he gave me his presence. My wife and I decided to leave academia and move to Georgia to be a full-time dad to my three children. I did not how I was going to earn a living, yet my wife and I started a small cleaning company and we worked day and night and in ten years I turned it into a multimillion dollar national and international company. One day at the heights of our company, making millions of dollars, it dawned on me that my children did not need me to make more millions. They needed what my dad gave me, my presence and in the heights of our company, at the age of 56 I called it quits and retired. I would now give my children what they truly needed - not yachts, or planes, but my presence. This time around was so different as my soul desire is to give back to others, to make a difference in the world, so I chose to dedicate my life to helping others, to share a message of hope, redemption, of a God who forgives, a message that we are not defined by our past, we can change if we want it bad enough. Today I send thousands of books to prisoners across America, to the many young people, women, men, forgotten by society, yet loved by Jesus. A message that if Jorge Valdes could change, anyone can change.

When I was featured on Netflix - Cocaine Cowboys, Kings of Miami, I prayed that after they showed a wild, exotic life that even many in the past died or are spending the rest of their lives in prison, that I would show great amount of change and forgiveness of sin. We see a show like that, and people are enamored by Narcos. I wish I had never heard of Narcos in my life again. I didn't really want to do this show because it shows a great amount glitter, but the producers and Netflix did an amazing job of letting the world see that many in the Kings of Miami, suffered a lot of pain, anguish and death. I am extremely regretful, and I wish I never did what I did, and I wish I could take it back and rewrite my story. I don't do what I do today to make up for what I did, I do it because I feel it is what God has called me to do to give somebody hope and so no other young man will become Jorge Valdes.

I pray that history remembers me not because of who I was or what I did, but simply, because I made a difference in someone's life.

E jvaldes@narcomindset.com
W www.narcomindset.com
W www.jorgevaldesphd.com

KEITH MEYER

DON'T WAIT UNTIL ITS TOO LATE
THE DAY I FORGAVE MY FATHER

"Childhood trauma runs deep. The day I forgave my father was the liberating moment, the breakthrough, which allowed my tortured life to finally find peace. In many ways it changed the way I thought, acted, and enabled me to know that I could finally move forward."

In general, we men are notoriously bad at showing and communicating our feelings. Unlike women, we tend to bottle up and hide our sensitivity and any form of weakness in front of our partners, colleagues, family, and close friends. All too often we do so at our own peril and, believe it or not, our physical and, in particular, our mental health suffers. We men, as a whole, have become masters at the big charade; "we're great, we're fine, all good, we say," when often inside we are consumed with anger, frustration, hurt, emotional pain, feelings of inadequacy and lack of self-esteem. We never admit to it or talk about with our partners and friends and colleagues as that would mean, as I said earlier, be portraying a weakness or sensitivity that is considered by society as just not manly.

My story is an in-depth account of PTSD and how long it took me to unravel from childhood trauma, the cause, 'deep rejection and alienation from my father' which had a crushing, compounding, and limiting impact on the rest of my life. That was until the day when I finally 'let it all out' that which I had been bottling up for so many years. In that instant I experienced a lightbulb moment which you will read about later. One where I felt the weight of the world finally lift off my shoulders. I hope that by reading it along with the other chapters of this book, you will come to understand that it is okay to feel vulnerable and show your feelings to anyone who will listen, and that by doing so you will be encouraged not to wait until it's too late and to seek help and overcome what can otherwise be a soul-destroying life-long experience.

Not that long ago I met up with a person I had known for a long time, someone I thought I knew well. He was in his early sixties and seemed fragile and on edge, so I asked him to tell me what it was that was bothering him. I had much soul reflection to do and in fact this person was me. I was talking to myself. I had a lot of past to unravel starting from the beginning of my life and how it came to be that my Dutch parents migrated to Australia in 1950, having lived for most of the preceding 27 years in Indonesia which was then under Dutch colonial rule. My parents had arrived in Sydney with my older sister in early May 1950. I was born on June 3, 1950, and was glad that I could proudly call myself an Australian.

However, from the age of five when I started school on the northern beaches side of Sydney and until my parents moved to Auckland, New Zealand when I was eight years old, I had gone to four different schools and from birth had lived in five different homes. My father was someone who found it hard to settle in his work and was always looking for new horizons. If I had to describe him, he was a person who worked hard and long hours and as a result did not spend much time with us his children as most fathers do or should do. After four years in New Zealand, my father, who was overweight and suffering from heart issues, had decided to take the family back to his native Holland in case anything did go wrong, so we would be able to get support from family.

I need you to understand what my life has been about all these years and what has been driving me to tell this story. While I didn't realise it at the time, my nomadic lifestyle had not only had a profound effect on my schooling thus far, but the fact that I had no bond with my father, as a father and son should have, had an even deeper and lasting effect on my ability to develop relationships with school friends.

I thought the Dutch language my parents had spoken while together at home all these years would arm me with the skills of fluency, but nothing could have been further from the truth, not to mention that I couldn't read or write it either. Upon arriving in Holland at the age of twelve when I should have started high school, I was forced to repeat a year and play catch-up with the language, as well as the history and geography of Europe.

I felt that my father's cavalier attitudes to seeking solace in his own life had forced a huge burden to be put on him, and I resented that. To make matters worse, my father seemed to delight in reminding me that, if I didn't meet the grades he expected, that I was destined for the lowest paid jobs and career path in the future. My anger and resentment towards my father was growing, but rather than standing up for myself, Keith Meyer became withdrawn and was rapidly and dangerously losing his self-esteem.

Too young to comprehend at the time I couldn't make sense of the way my father was so distant and the way he acted but given his own upbringing and the extreme trauma he had faced in his own life, It made a lot of sense. He had left home at the age of fourteen to escape his own father who was an abusive alcoholic. After marrying my mother, they decided to try their luck in The Dutch East Indies as they were then known. He worked as a tailor by trade, and they lived a charmed and prosperous life in the colonial tropical paradise, with lots of parties and few cares.

Then just before the beginning of World War II when Japan invaded Indonesia, they had been blessed with a daughter, Edith. She tragically died due to malnutrition in a prisoner of war camp on Java at the age of two and a half while interned with my mother just four months before the war ended. It was 1944. My father had been captured on Java and shipped to Changi, prisoner of war camp on the Island of Singapore, so he and my mother were both separated in that time for four and a half years with no contact. Three years later, my mother gave birth to another daughter Alice and three years later I was born.

A distinct moment that stands out for me was when I was in my final year at high school in Utrecht, Holland. One evening over dinner at home with my family my father announced that he and my mother had decided to move back to Sydney, Australia again, as he had been offered a job by a previous employer in women's fashion, who had tracked him down. The question was put to me by my father – did I want to stay in Holland with my sister who was already engaged and about to be married, or did I want to go back to Australia? With three more schools in Holland to my tally and two more moves in five years, I once again bade my school friends adieu and, with scant regard to maintaining contact with any of them – something that I had sadly conditioned myself to doing with all the times I had moved – I headed back to the country I had always called home, Australia.

In recollection my father and I had never been close, as in a father-son sense. I can recall a great deal of my early childhood such as street names and numbers of places I lived, but there were no memories of father-son times kicking a ball in the backyard or going fishing or playing in a park. I had tried to come to accept that my father may not have had much of the same with his own father. Add to that the number of hours my dad worked and the fact that my parents were both forty years old when I was born, they were often too tired to do anything.

My sister on the other hand, who in later years had chosen fashion design as a career path, was closer with my father than I was. I can remember a particular spate of hurtful and consistent putdowns by my father regarding my school results, causing me to even ask my mother at the age of thirteen if I was adopted because I couldn't believe a father would be so vitriolic and nasty to a real son who was trying so hard. In order to remove myself from the pain and rejection,

I used to take long bicycle rides by myself on weekends to escape from his gaze and unending critique and often wondered if anyone would really care if I just disappeared and didn't come home. I feel embarrassed to tell you that I had, between the ages of thirteen and seventeen, contemplated suicide on a number of occasions.

When I arrived back in Sydney in June 1967, at the age of seventeen, my mood had changed and the veil that had shrouded me in that terrible time of self-harm and suicidal ideation had lifted as I had hope in the fact that I had secured myself a great job within four days of arriving back. Even though it was an administration job at Fiat Motors Spare Parts, I finally felt like I was achieving some independence. I had money in the bank as I had brought with me just over AUD $2000 (a lot of money for those times), the proceeds of savings from my weekend car-cleaning business which I had been operating in Holland from the time I was fifteen years old. An old family acquaintance soon offered me a bigger job in the claims department of a large insurance company and, with lots of overtime on offer, I was able to buy a car and take the girl I had since met out on dates. Life was great.

I had met Virginia, a hairdresser, late in 1967 and married her in 1973, and we are still together today. When I agreed to return to Sydney with my father in June, I had some reservations about how he and I would get along together. My mother followed in the October of the same year after finalising the sale of their apartment in Holland and arranging for the packing and shipping of all our belongings. One day, my father who had never been violent in the past towards me in any way – abusive yes, but never violent, out of nowhere hit me twice across the back of the head which sent me reeling. This sudden outburst of aggression was due to something I apparently said that had angered my father, whether by disagreeing with him or by the way I had spoken to him.

I had resolved to keep out of his way by making myself scarce and enjoying my time away from my father's company. Nearly two years after arriving back in Sydney in July 1969, while my mother was overseas visiting my sister who had not long given birth to her first child, my father asked me one Sunday morning if he could borrow my car, as his had a flat battery. I dived into my trouser pocket for the keys, gave them to him and asked, "where are you off to and what time will you be home?" He replied, "out to lunch with some friends and I should be home around 4pm," as he shut the door behind him.

They were the last words we ever spoke to each other. At approximately 3pm there was a knock at the door, which upon opening revealed two large police officers from the local police station, who asked if this was my father's residence, and who I was. They then proceeded to tell me that my father had passed away in a guest house in the inner city of Sydney and was found in bed with a woman who had reported his death to the authorities. It took a long while for me to gather my composure and process the information that I had just heard. I had just turned nineteen and, while it is commonly accepted that young men don't mature till the right frontal lobe of their brain develops fully at between twenty-three to twenty-five years of age, in that moment, I felt like I had just been forced to grow up very suddenly.

The Police, who had since left, had told me I would have to go to Central Sydney Police station in the CBD to sign some papers, take charge of my father's personal belongings, and be taken to the Morgue for official identification. I walked upstairs and, after I explained to my neighbour what had just happened the neighbour offered to drive me into the Central Sydney Police. With the formalities there completed and with the envelope with my father's belongings – watch, wallet, spectacles and some money etc – in a brown paper bag, some young officers then took me down to the City Morgue where I was asked to officially identify my father's body. A task I did with little or no true understanding of what the ramifications of the events of this day would have on the rest of my life.

As I recount and recall these moments, my emotions get the better of me and talking about these memories are very painful, even though they happened so long ago. Even though I feel as though I want to stop here and continue on at another time, I am so glad that I have found someone, you the reader, to talk to and tell my story, which I have bravely, if not in a damaging way, held onto for so long.

I remember as I viewed my father's cold and grey body lying on the mortuary slab, my legs went out from under me, and the two young constables who must have anticipated something grabbed me under the armpits and held me upright as I nodded my head to the question, "Is this your father?" and "Please state the name of the deceased to identify him." Kindly, the officers then drove me, still numb as if in shock, back to the area where my father had passed away, and they started looking in the surrounding streets for his car. It was quickly located. I was now starting to focus on the realities and ramifications of what had happened and began thinking of the steps that needed to be taken.

I waited until about 6 pm to call my sister to deliver the tragic news, which meant it was early morning in Holland. I knew I would be asked how our father had died and where. What would I say? More to the point, what could I say that would not hurt my mother and my sister and the rest of the family? I knew that telling my mother the truth would mean adding further stress to the grief she would already have to suffer, and it would leave her with lifelong questions unanswered. I calmly explained to my sister that our father, who had a known heart condition, had suffered a massive heart attack as a passenger in the car while I was driving, and that it was all over in a matter of seconds.

The ensuing conversations with my mother, brother-in-law and sister were all about consoling them but strangely I didn't feel sad, just betrayed. Betrayed by my father who was always so self-righteous about what was right and what was wrong, and about being honest.

It was only thanks to the support and thoughtfulness of my girlfriend, that I was able to somehow assemble my life back together and move on as best I could at the time, managing to create a successful career - believe it or not in the women's fashion industry. This all came about after my father's passing, when the company he had worked for on his return to Australia asked me to join them in a sales capacity.

On the home front my wife was in her own hairdressing salon which she started in 1972 and later sold in order to start a family. We had a son, Christian who was born in 1975, a daughter, Jessica in 1977, and another daughter Nicola in 1979. All through the ensuing years, life was hectic. My own work commitments and busy schedules meant I spent the best part of twenty-two years travelling up to six - seven months of the year away on business trips, sales and marketing campaigns, although home on most weekends.

However, whenever the tyranny of distance meant too much lost time, I stayed away for two weeks. Looking back, it seemed as though when I was away working and while I was in my sales role, I was 'on my stage', in my emotional high zone. But when the day was finished and I was eating alone in a restaurant or watching television in my hotel suite, I found myself depressed and alone with no one to talk to.

Clearly having been what I had been through there was a lot underneath the surface which I just put to the back of my mind and tried to block out the pain, as all men do. I found writing to my mother difficult; over time my guilt and the burden of honesty had become worse since I had visited Holland in December 1984 with my son. When my sister had asked late one evening if I had ever visited our father's grave, I answered no, and there and then I decided to spill out to her and her husband what had been burdening my for the last fifteen years.

I guess at the time I was expecting sympathy and understanding from them but I did not get it. Instead, my sister told me that she wasn't surprised that our father had done that, and after my sister had left the room and gone to bed, my brother-in-law said to me, he thought I was a strange person for having told my sister the truth about our father and damaging her memories of him forever.

As I recall this I still solemnly shake my head in defeat and disbelief and mutter to myself, "I was damned if I did and damned if I didn't." Needless to say, the last few days of that visit were very tense and unpleasant, and I felt that even thought it had been fifteen years after his death I was still there being haunted and tortured.

One thing I did seek assurance on before departing was that my sister and brother-in-law would keep in confidence what had been discussed, and never tell our mother, seventy-four years old at the time, so as to let her live out her years in peace. I was grateful that they had kept this confidence and my mum died peacefully in her sleep in October 2010, at the glorious age of ninety-nine years and ten months without ever knowing the hurtful truth.

Despite this assurance, and my belief that it would never be divulged, I spoke to my doctor about my emotions and the issues that were weighing hard on my heart. The doctor suggested that I see a psychiatrist to help resolve any issues that were obviously still bothering me mentally. Several visits later and some excellent therapy by the psychiatrist led to a session of outpouring of unresolved grief when the doctor suggested that I tell my father (using a photo that he asked me to bring along) exactly what I had been bottling up all these years.

In just over an hour, I went through an entire box of tissues as I vented all of my pent-up anger and frustration towards the image of my father on the chair opposite me. I felt utterly exhausted and relieved at the same time when it was over. To describe that moment – It would have been unpleasant to watch but it was so good after a few days, when the effect had sunk in, to know that all that unresolved hatred, anger, frustration, hurt and grief had finally come out.

One day, very shortly after this therapy session, whilst sitting on a park bench, I had an extraordinary lightbulb moment. I realised deep within my soul, that in order to see myself totally free and able to move on completely, that I needed to take the step to forgive my father. This was the liberating moment, the breakthrough, which allowed my tortured life to finally find peace. In many ways it changed the way I thought, acted, and enabled me to know that I could finally move forward.

To all of the people out there reading this, my life story, I would like to assure you of the strength and courage it took me to write it and share it with you. I also commend you all as men or women to talk to professional people that can help you overcome the hurdles of your life that have become barriers. Feelings that have emanated through events in life have a propensity to linger on and become like wounds that won't heal unless treated and resolved. I know that much of what I have suffered over a large part of my life could have been avoided if those around me had suggested I seek help earlier.

This story is but one part of my journey through life; I could write more about the loss of our son at the young age of twenty-four years and eleven months, surviving a near-death experience in a car accident at fifty-four years of age, and losing our cherished home a year later. I could write about receiving the diagnosis of Bi-Polar II disorder (something I probably have had all my life) at the age of sixty, to add to the MDD Major Depressive Disorder and Anxiety, all of which I have learned to function and live with normally. It just goes to show that you're not dead till the lid closes and the lights go out, and until then anything and everything is possible.

I am a born communicator, a person who has a strong moral and social compass and who is in my element while listening to and helping others who have been demoralized and afflicted or aggrieved by the actions of others. This no doubt comes in part from my own life's experiences, dealing with depression and anxiety as well as his numerous roles and vast management experience in the business world. Today I am a mentor and teacher to many who don't have the years of wisdom and hindsight to draw on that I have had.

KEITH MEYER – Corporate Management Trainer – Business and Personal Mentor – Speaker – Author
keithvmeyer@gmail.com

MASON HOPE

MUSICIAN AND MENTAL HEALTH AMBASSADOR
FOR THE YOUTH OF TODAY

OVERCOMING REJECTION TO BUILD
MY DREAMS

"In that lightbulb moment as I stood before a crowded room sharing my story for the very first time at the age of 12, suddenly, I knew I deserved happiness."

I was born on the Sunshine Coast in August of 1999, and I am from a Cook Island background. It was a time of turbulence between my mother and father. This continued for the first six months of my life, at which time my father left without looking back. My mother became ill and couldn't care for me. So, by my first birthday, I was living with and being raised by my grandmother Lisa. Unprepared for a small child my nan as I call her, quickly adjusted her life to care for me.

My childhood has many happy memories for me, but they are intertwined with trauma and abandonment issues. My nan always gave me lots of love, doing everything she could do to bring me happiness. But she struggled to work while suffering herself with increasing health issues. She has been there for me in every way, and I love her for that. However, physically and financially we struggled.

I was a very lonely kid with no one to do those things younger parents do - running and kicking a ball, bike riding, surfing at the beach. Nan had no friends with children my age and was limited because of health issues. I really missed not having a father. I had paternal grandparents and paternal aunties living close by, but they were not really interested. A few visited me around age 10 more out of curiosity, and then disappeared. This left me feeling abandoned again and again. Why didn't they stay in my life? Why didn't they love me?

Primary school was a battering of bullying from about grade 4 up. I would come home and lay in the yard and cry. There was a particularly cruel taunt which was "your parents hate you and that's why they don't see you." I was excluded from play and when I tried to speak there was a group who would make noises, shutting me down, shutting me out. I was pushed around, and every day was a Groundhog Day of misery. My nan tried to work with the school but looking back now I feel the system was broken. At that time, I went and saw a paediatrician who diagnosed me with depression and anxiety. I was having panic attacks daily leading to asthma attacks. I was 11 years old. I saw councillors but had already begun to shut down, I thought no one wanted me. Even though Nan was a huge support for me and gave me lots of love and made a happy home for us, I still felt the rejection of abandonment.

Nan had been trying to find my father and had been doing so for years. Every year nan would do a search for him through all the phone directories. We eventually found him through my grandfather who still showed no interest in being in my life. Nan invited my father to visit with the only condition that if he came back into my life he would stay. My father visited me when I was around nine. He visited my home, took me to the park and I even asked him to come to the school for just one afternoon, so everyone could see he was there for me. He was leaving to go to Adelaide. Before he left he promised to keep in touch and said, "I'll call you Monday." I didn't hear from him. He didn't return my calls; I was crushed. A year later he turned up as if nothing had been wrong. It was confusing but I still wanted his love and acceptance. When he was leaving again for Adelaide the second time, he gave me a mobile phone. He said this would make it easier for us to keep in contact. The phone was in his name and he would pay for the account. After he left he never returned my calls and after one month the mobile phone was disconnected. I cried so much. I was just a young boy. My anger was mounting.

I didn't hear from my father again for ten years. His rejection had hit me hard; I was an angry little guy. My father was a DJ and one of my school friends befriended him on Facebook. I was mortified and embarrassed as my friend knew more about him than I did. I sent my father a Facebook friendship request, which he accepted. This was such a mistake - it was more of the same, being ignored and now on a social media platform. In that time I watched him get married and announce the birth of his sons via social media, the posting of his children making him so happy; they were the best thing that ever happened to him. I wasn't crying anymore. I was numb, with anger. Many emotions began bubbling under the surface.

Years later when I sang on the TV show 'The Voice' in 2018, he contacted me, he wanted to share my music and achievements with his friends. He said he was proud of me. I asked him to leave me alone. It was so upsetting to think that this was what it took for him to notice me. I had a panic attack. I knew I couldn't survive being rejected again. A moment that should have brought me joy, ended with me shutting down in terrible anxiety and depression.

My mother was around here and there during my young life and when I was twelve years old, she gave birth to my brother. My brother and I are very close, and I see him often. My mother has shown support for me in my teenage years, and we see each other regularly now.

I have three half-brothers in total, two I've never met in person, who are my father's children. Eventually he left them too, this saddened me greatly. What I have learnt over the years is my father had been raised by his grandmother, also his father, my grandfather was raised by his grandmother. A cycle of parental abandonment.

When I entered high school, a situation came about where my grandmother was obtaining a school bus pass. My surname is unusual and the lady at the bus company said to nan, we have a bus driver that has the same name. My grandmother said yes that's Masons grandfather, but they have no relationship. Though nan had rung my grandfather over the years, and he lived literally five minutes away he wasn't interested in getting to know me. The lady said to nan, I hope that's not a problem because he will be your grandsons bus driver. Nan struggled with telling me but thought I should know in case he approached me. When giving out the bus passes, he called out my name which he knew but said nothing. I sat on that bus for nearly a year without any recognition from him. Another rejection which was hard for me.

Internalising my pain once again, Nan called my grandfather and spoke to him about how I was feeling. He started seeing me a few times but after a while he told us it bothered his children. I haven't seen him for some years now.

As I entered high school, I read an article about 'Headspace' and filled in an application to join the 'Headspace Maroochydore Youth Engagement committee'. I was successful. At that point I was twelve and became the youngest member to join their committee. Headspace provides early intervention mental health support for young people aged twelve to twenty-five. I loved being around these good and kind people, while also being educated to be part of the solution for kids like me. I actually was part of the team that picked the furnishing and wall colours to be used at Headspace Maroochydore. I was honoured to be asked to emcee the event which was the opening of our local Headspace and sing a few songs.

There was a moment as I reached the end of my official duties as emcee, for this very special event. As I made my final speech, I spoke from my personal story sharing my life, and what I hoped for, and these words have stuck with me over the years since then. "*I just want every kid out there like me to know that there is a way through this and to reach out because there are people who will listen and help and if I can do it so can you and when you do it's a beautiful thing.*" In speaking those words out loud to a packed audience of media, and mental health and youth health professionals, I felt a sudden release of pain and I was flooded with joy and hope. At twelve years old speaking these words out loud was the most defining moment of my young life. It was a lightbulb moment where suddenly '*I knew I deserved happiness*'. This realisation would have the greatest impact on my personal wellbeing and go on to pave the path of my career.

From this moment I felt the pressure lift and I was full of hope. It was from this point onwards that my life changed. Suddenly knowing I deserved happiness; the right people started to come into my life. My amazing music teachers who believed in me and nurtured my talent. New opportunities in my music career came along which I felt confident to explore and led to many great and memorable moments in my life.

I continued my journey with Headspace and have been a volunteer there now for over 11 years, exactly half my life. I have been both a local member and a national member of Headspace, joining the Headspace Youth National high energy team and receiving training in Melbourne. Since joining the team at the age of 12, I have shared my story now with many mental health campaigns including Beyond Blue targeting anxiety, speaking, and singing at the national Headspace Day conference in Melbourne, R U OK? Trust the Signs tour. What I find wonderful, is that people of all ages will approach me afterwards and will open up and reach out. It gives me such a great feeling to know there is help out there and I can help people find that help.

Through my years in school, I had been learning the drums, followed by the guitar and then as a vocalist. In 2016 I had a big year and was accepted into the Creative Generations state schools onstage as a featured vocalist. In the same year I entered and won the Voice of Urban talent search, followed by entering and winning the National and Iconic Gympie Muster national talent search. As part of the prize, I was flown over to Norfolk Island in 2017 to compete in and also win The Trans-Tasman Entertainer of The Year. One of the judges Shane Nicholson is a multi-award-winning artist and producer, whom I now work with as he produces my music.

I have been fortunate to play at some amazing festivals Bluesfest, Gympie Muster, Caloundra Music Festival, Norfolk Island. My latest music releases have made apple playlists and no 1 on iTunes charts also making the Apra and AMRAP charts. This has allowed me to have a platform to share my story and encourage other young people to pursue their passion and not give up. That my story may encourage another young persons to not give up is my greatest achievement. Pain and anxiety still raises its head from time to time and anxiety can bubble below the surface, but now I have a hold of the problem and have the tools, the confidence, and the mindset to get through it.

Today I seek to find a balance in my life, I have no problem with assessing my time and giving my mental health a priority. I have the self-worth and confidence to say no to things and people that may cause unneeded pressure. I am aware I still have some emotional triggers, but I feel the years following my "lightbulb" moment have allowed me to accept that I deserve happiness and healing. And if life throws me a curly one, I know I can reach out. To me reaching out when needed is key to a good mental health plan, also knowing it's ok to not feel ok sometimes. I stand by those words that I said many years ago "If I can do it, so can you." I reflect on these words, and they give me peace.

I think we may all be given a chance at or struck by the 'lightbulb' moment, but it seems to be those who have lived through pain or trauma in their life, may be the ones who lock in and seize the moment with both hands as I did. The epiphany, the defining moment, the lightbulb moment, I was so fortunate to have, gave me a defining realization, so young. I sincerely hope that everyone has their lightbulb moment and uses it to find their way through any trial or sadness they may be experiencing toward a greater life than ever before.

www.masonhope.com.au

MICHAEL GALLUS

FOUNDER FOOTY'S 4 ALL

THE SCHOOL TEACHER STEPPING OUT OF THE COMFORT ZONE - CHANGING KIDS LIVES GLOBALLY BY BRINGING HOPE - ONE FOOTY AT A TIME

"The ability to forget your struggles and challenges by running around with a footy by yourself or with your family or mates bringing joy through the power of sport, is 'life changing'".

"How boring would life be if you never took risks or broke the safe mould that you built around yourself. Life is not about success and failure but the way you handle each of those situations and the emotions that go with it.

A day in the last few years, a lightbulb moment propelled me to change direction. This has since sparked a series of flashing strobe light bulb moments which has seen my direction rapidly changing in every which way. Something which is indicative of many people's lives in these ever changing and fluid times since the Covid crisis, especially here where I live in Melbourne, Australia. During these uncertain times of direction in my life, it is important to state that the constants for me have been my faith in God, the love and support from my wife Amanda, my children - Tom, Lily, and Ben, along with my Mum and Dad, three brothers and extended family and my wide circle of friends from across Australia, Fiji, and Pakistan. They have enabled me to reach out for support when times were tough and continue to move forward in a positive light regardless of the challenges and uncertainty that I have faced.

Have I realised that life is shortening, and it is imperative that I try to experience every aspect of it I can, or is it because of, or as well as the fact that I am in a position of being mentally strong, with great support, to now step outside my lane? Am I totally erratic or is their method in the madness and how and by what do you measure these changes as successful? Do you have a successful change if you earn lots of money and improve your

knowledge or is it a combination of a variety of reasons all
stemming from the ideal that it is ok to fail and not achieve any
of your success criteria? Are these similar reasons that you have
found for your ability to follow through with a lightbulb
moment or moments?

Well, smack bang in the middle of my life after a moment of
inspiration, a lightbulb moment propelled me into my greatest
purpose ever!

It was after hearing a moving speech by the inspirational
South African leader, Nelson Mandela as he stated the following
at the Laureus Sports Awards in 2000, he said, "*sport has the
power to change the world'. It has the power to inspire. It has
the power to unite people in a way that little else does. It speaks
to youth in a language they understand. Sport can create hope
where once there was only despair. It is more powerful than
governments in breaking down racial barriers. It laughs in the
face of all types of discrimination.*" He then proved his words
true by uniting his country through the triumph of winning the
1995 Rugby Union World Cup in his home country of South
Africa. It was these words and deeds by Mr. Mandela that
inspired me with the idea to create the children's volunteer
sporting charity, 'Footys4all'.

I had just turned 40 years of age and in my moment of mid-
life crisis I decided that instead of buying the red sports car that
I would start a charity. I decided after being a life-long fan of

Nelson Mandela, to try to put his words into action and use all my contacts that I had come to know through fifteen years of community sports coaching in the AGSV competition/Aberfeldie FC's Auskick and Junior Football Program, AFL radio and Television Commentary and teaching at two local Grammar Schools, to start my charity.

I had been blessed throughout my life through my own education and teaching career at P.E.G.S. to see the power of sport and its impact that it had on me, my students, my children, and my community. I saw the way that training and playing sport taught the participants resilience, courage, teamwork, preparation, commitment, passion, dedication, success and failure, discipline, inclusion, and respect just to name a few. I was sick and tired of seeing children who loved their sport missing out on its joys mainly due to reasons such as socio economic and living in remoteness. I wanted to create an impact that would allow these children around Australia to gain the same opportunities to engage in sporting activities that everyone else had. I had also seen the positive mental health aspects of playing sports. Now playing sports doesn't just mean joining a team. Playing sports can mean kicking a soccer or football by yourself around your backyard or out in the street with the neighbors'. My definition of playing sport is playing sport both organised and free spirited.

Playing sport is so good for your mental and physical health at all ages but especially for kids and especially for kids doing it tough financially, in remote locations or in a foreign location. The ability to forget your struggles and challenges by running around with a ball by yourself or with your family or with your mates bringing joy through the power of sport is life changing. I have been blessed to spend time in many remote aboriginal communities and the joy that sport brings to the kids on the Tiwi Islands, on Noonkanbah Cattle Station, on Elcho Island and across the outback is unparalleled to any other life experience apart from them watching their favourite teams playing in community or on TV. Feeling good about yourself and creating an enjoyable experience with your friends and family blocks out the challenges of living hundreds of kilometers from anyone and anywhere in droughts and flooding rains. How did you feel as a kid kicking that imaginary goal to win the game after the siren in the backyard? I certainly felt on top of the world!

The spark which lit the fire already burning within me for Footy's4 all, happened at Aberfeldie Auskick when a young boys dad donated $3,000 to a fundraiser organised by two other prominent people in the footy community at Aberfeldie Auskick for an upgrade in equipment. They asked that I spend $1000 of his donation in providing equipment to kids doing it tough. I knew of friends and family working in remote areas of the Northern Territory and Outback WA and purchased footballs and basketballs and sent them off. Upon receiving the photos of the kids with huge smiles on their faces and the joy it created I had a light bulb moment and thought it was time with the great team around me that I tried to make a difference and provide sporting opportunities for all kids no matter what their socio-economic status or living location in life.

10 years later and thanks to an army of volunteers and the following sponsors-TNT, Nissan, Ross Faukner, Steeden and Gilbert, Winsher Sports, The Bresnahan Footprint Foundation, Blaze Acumen, Kennards Self Storage, Blue Swan Clothing and supporters around Australia, Fiji, Pakistan and around the world, led first and foremost by my amazing family of Amanda, Thomas, Lily and Ben Gallus, 27,000 new Footys4all footballs, rugby balls, basketballs, soccer balls and volleyballs, have been distributed all through private donations. Despite 10 years of state and federal political grant meetings for ZERO contribution from our taxpayer money that should be used funding sporting programs like Footys4all for kids in need instead of the billions wasted on cancelled transport, submarine, defence dealings.

Thank God for the generous human beings and businesses who understand the power of sport and impact that Footys4all makes on those who are doing it tough. Together we will march on and continue to do all we can do to keep spreading Footys around the globe. The power of sport through Footys4all has changed lives and delivered hope to those recipients in Juvenile Justice Centre's, maximum security prisons, remote aboriginal communities, special needs and low socioeconomic schools, sporting clubs and charities across Australia and beyond, but I never forget that Footys4all is only possible due to a team effort and nothing is able to be done without the grace of God, my beautiful family and the greatest army of Footys4all volunteers, sponsors and supporters one could ever ask for.

Do you think that lightbulb moments are moments which only occur due to our prior based experiences giving us the confidence to change our journey or making us change our path due to the extreme situation we are in? Or is it our internal fate or survival mode instincts or both? When Covid struck two years ago, the situation certainly became extreme. At that time when the world was on hold and my job as a high school teacher came to a halt, and travelling for Footys4All became impossible, a new direction was needed. It was another lightbulb moment which led me to run for the local council election. This time my inspiration came after being involved in many council volunteer community sporting committees over the prior years and lobbying for many sporting issues such as ensuring that the council didn't close the East Keilor Leisure Centre outdoor 50m pool and gaining goal posts and proper changing room facilities for the East Keilor FC first ever female football team. I wanted to make a difference.

Was I nervous, worried, unsure about this totally new change of direction and the possibility of publicly falling flat on my face with not enough votes to make a good account of myself? You betcha, bottom dollar! Did it matter? Not to me or my supporters as one of my philosophies in life is 'never be afraid to fail' as it is the journey that is important, not the result you wish for yourself. So, I figured I had nothing to lose by stepping out. Regardless of whether or not you achieve your success criteria, your learning will still be utmost as you have ventured outside your norm which will teach you a great deal more about yourself. You will learn how you react to new challenges and how resilient you really are especially when things are not going as expected in your chosen direction towards where you believe your lightbulb moment is leading you. You never know if your new sideways path will eventually lead you to your goal or create an opportunity for a different light bulb moment. Life is about feeling valued and valuing yourself enough to have a go.

Now in 2022, Footys4all is rippling around the world. Next week I head off to Pakistan to spread a bit of hope to the kids over in that part of the world. And, it all started with a light bulb moment! And one that changed my life and inspired me to impact the physical and mental health of all recipients not just through the power of a ball but through the emotion of hope. Every Footys4all recipient has been grateful to gain an opportunity to play sport, but they also realised that the thousands of people involved with Footys4all care about them enough to do all this work to provide them with a sporting opportunity. That fact provides all Footys4all ball recipients with a spark of hope to continue on despite their tough circumstances and not to give up on their dreams what-ever they maybe. And you know what sometimes in life that's all you need-a little hope.

Footys4all it is not rocket science just Footys4all thanks to all your support.

Michaelggallus@gmail.com

MICHAEL RAY

SOLO DAD AT 49

SUDDENLY ILL, SUDDENLY SINGLE, SUDDENLY A DAD

"At forty-nine and becoming a dad, my male bravado disappeared in a flurry of nappies, bows, and pretty dresses. I've never felt so vulnerable and unsure yet so grateful at the same time."

Who knew that my Lightbulb moment would be the gift of clarity that hit me square between the eyes, bestowed upon me through a crisis that would see me re - emerging as a better human, not disconnected from my pre - crisis self, more as though I had been shattered into a thousand pieces and suddenly, completely, and permanently reassembled into a sentient and grateful dad.

It had it's beginning in an accidental crisis, one that I'm forever grateful for. Even if in my juvenile male manner of dealing with crisis, I reverted to gung-ho humour and smart-arse retorts to deal with the news.

It all culminated and came crashing down one night. My personal life was in shambles. My health was suffering physically and mentally, and my energy levels were at an all-time low. It was completely understandable though, right?

I had been working like a mad man to provide for my new family and wanting to be the best, most hands-on dad EVER. I wanted to be involved in all the minutia of raising my daughter. I absolutely loved everything about it — the night feeds, the nappy changes, bath time and bedtime, because that's what a good dad does, right? A real man, a real dad, puts his family first and any thought of seeing one of those doctor thingy's would just have to wait. (Insert alpha male chest pounding and grunting here!)

My relatively short, although important, relationship with my six-month-old daughter's mother had ended a couple of weeks earlier and in that time, I hadn't seen my daughter who I'd waited my entire forty-nine years to be blessed with. Strange, isn't it? Forty-nine years without this kid and suddenly a day apart from her was almost unbearable.

I decided that I needed a night out; a distraction to drag me out of the dark recesses of my mind. Adding some alcohol seemed like the perfect route to the resolution of my physical and mental malaise, right? (Insert more chest pounding and grunting here) And what a good night it turned out to be. In fact, it was that good it didn't end for a couple of nights as was the fashionable trend of my excessive youth. But like all good things, they must end. I found myself waking up in a haze at a stranger's house and after a full day and into the evening of awkward, trivial conversation, biding my time to ensure I was sober enough to flee, I got into my car and started my trip home.

As I listened to the great tunes, slowly the temporary distance I had put between myself, and my thoughts dissipated. I let reality pour over me with my attention suddenly snapped back to the present and the dog in my path. The 'don't swerve' advice that we are given was forgotten. As a lover of animals, there was no way I was going to add to my brilliant list of failures by killing a helpless animal. I hit the brakes. The dog froze in the headlights, like a deer. There was no stopping now and there was only one option that didn't involve a dead or damaged dog. I swerved. BANG! I hit a tree.

I swear the dog was laughing at me, and life, once again, was giving me the middle finger, or vice versa, maybe even both. The dog hastily departed the scene without the slightest pretence of going for help, as was the legend of the much-revered Lassie.

The tree was conveniently located directly across from a convenience store and not so conveniently lodged firmly in the front of my car. The dear souls on duty witnessed the whole accident and called for an ambulance. After much arm waiving, bad jokes, and reassurances that I was fine, I relented and decided to get a free ride to the hospital. After all, my car was not going anywhere, and I had lost any hope the dog was returning to promise me his first-born son would be named in my honour for saving his ungrateful life.

After being quizzed, prodded, poked and breathalysed, I arrived at the hospital and was wheeled off to wait for the inevitable cursory examination. With my obvious extensive medical knowledge, gathered from years of near miss hospital visits and selected TV medical shows, led me to conclude with relative certainty, was unnecessary and I would soon be released with a sense of guilt for wasting everyone's time to add to my list of growing achievements.

For some reason my mind had decided now was the perfect time to compile a chronological highlight reel of every failure, stupid decision, and self-inflicted near-death experience I had made throughout my colourful and eventful life, complete with narration by someone who sounded incredibly like Morgan Freeman — alas, it was not he.

The initial vigour had died down and I'd been downgraded from emergency to procedural check-up after 'concerns' were raised by the attending physician. I was lying in the hospital room, surrounded by the silence of an early morning hospital, waiting for the CAT scan. In the silence, one tends to get lost in the valleys of the mind, you wonder around and look behind rocks and trees that you'd forgotten, or rather, had chosen to forget. I was still trying to come to terms with the separation of my marriage and not having seen my six-month-old daughter for what seemed like an eternity but in reality, was only a few weeks.

I will admit, on the surface, my best efforts at portraying that I was in good spirits was a façade that was hardly manageable even though I had been taught my entire life, 'Never let your opponent know you're hurt', and despite having spent a lifetime practicing and developing my male bravado I was suddenly feeling weak, even a little vulnerable. A tiredness that ran so deep it was hard to breath and made my heartbeat with a deafening rhythm that was reminiscent of a boxing match, the final round. I was completely gassed, unable to even hold my hands up to protect myself from my opponent's punches. Blow after blow landed as I stood in front of him like a punching bag with eyes. I took great comfort, even pride in the fact I wouldn't buckle or show any weakness to him or the crowd of spectators, yet here I lay in the quiet of the hospital scared, filled with a sense that life hadn't quite managed to knock me out, but had managed to punch me into submission. I wanted to quit. I felt that I was buckled and my ego, my pride, my bravado had thrown in the towel and deserted me.

It was an uncomfortable and confronting feeling. A lifetime of squashing everything down into that pit had suddenly exploded from the depths like an inflating raft, except this felt like it was going to drown me, rather than save me.

Looking back at this time, especially with the benefit of hindsight and my gift of clarity that this unfolding crisis had endowed me with, I lay there thinking about my daughter. To this day, thinking about Charlie makes me well up with emotion. Charlie, who was named after my dad, really was perfect to me, yet, somehow in the instant she came into this world, I knew intrinsically, and without doubt, I had to be better than the carefree Peter Pan that I had been until now. I'd had a colourful life — a life that makes my Mum blush and shake her head in disbelief. From being a burly bouncer and doorman by night, providing security for almost every local and international rock star that travelled to Australia; a bodybuilder and personal trainer by day, living it up in Melbourne's 80's and 90's. Being from this clique one realises that this lifestyle is one of fanciful excess granting complete disregard for the future. You think you're invincible, unstoppable, bulletproof.

Eventually I was wheeled in to have my CAT scan, a precaution I was told just to make sure that my neck was ok. There was no internal damage. As I waited for the doctor, I began to think about how this was another lucky escape like the other near misses I'd had.

The scan was simple and painless, and I'd had enough. I really just wanted to crawl into my own bed and get a good sleep before my day needed to start again. I walked out and caught a cab home.

I was in a deep sleep, enveloped by my warm blanket, when I became aware of a tiny but frantic voice calling my name accompanied by a tapping. The tapping got louder as did the voice, now bellowing my name. I woke up with a start, sitting bolt upright in my bed. Mum was standing in my doorway, pale and panicked.

"Michael," she scolded, "I've just got off the phone with the hospital. What is going on? They said you walked out. You need to go back. They're sending an ambulance!"

I woke fully at the word ambulance. I told mum to get my sister so she could run me to the hospital to see what all the hoo-ha was about. Bless my sister's soul, she's a good egg and did her sisterly duty of driving me and stopping for coffee and breakfast first.

After the flurry of paperwork and evil sideward glances from the nursing staff, I was shepherded in to see the doctor. He looked grave and serious, so serious in fact that my sister was asked to leave the room.

Once alone the doctor informed me that I was going to be admitted and required to stay for a week after telling me how lucky I was. Obviously, I had no clue what he was talking about. In my style, I mentioned something about this not being Club Med and that the coffee was sub-par.

He raised his eyebrow and proceeded to tell me that the Bilateral Pulmonary Embolism was his major concern and nearly the end of me. That it would have been me cashing in my ticket. So, if that was the major concern, what on earth were the minor concerns? I didn't have to wait long for a response.

They still had to assess to see if it was a surgical procedure or simply treatment that I required. The fact that the embolisms – yes, I did say embolisms – plural, were well formed and residing happily in my lungs, was the reason they wanted to keep an eye on me. Touch and go according to the professionals.

Apparently, the good news was that when these were addressed and treated, they would then proceed further to investigate the masses found in my brain, nodules in my lungs and the lymph node abnormalities. Besides that, I was in great health.

My sister eventually came back into the room after the doctor left to find me in a complete daze. There was sudden clarity. I had been feeling short-of-breath and generally under the weather, but I would never have guessed that this would be the issue. I honestly thought that I was just getting old and my carefree and happy life until now was taking its toll. It felt like the soundtrack to my life was beginning to end. For all my jokes and quips, I was scared; really scared.

After all, becoming a father so late in life was in itself a shock and until my daughter was born, I had no idea that a love so intense could ever exist – an all-consuming, overwhelming mix of fear of the unknown, and a sense of such intense pride that it sometimes makes my heart feel like it's going to explode. It's almost as though my life before was of no real consequence or significance, just all-in preparation.

With Charlie's mum and I ending our relationship coupled with the days that I'd not seen Charlie, the uncertainty of how this split would affect this newfound purpose and now the given diagnosis, it was safe to say that I was in crisis. My focus was drawn acutely onto what really matters versus the stories I'd been telling myself for years about what I thought mattered, was the gift.

My world had, in a split second, become my house that I'd built, furnished, and filled with a lifetime of effort, and in an instant there's flames leaping through the roof, and I had to consider what, if anything, was I prepared to rush in to try and save. What was replaceable, expendable or of no consequence? How much of my life, my energy and focus had been used up in acquiring these things? Most people, when I ask this question, reply with photos, keepsakes, basically memories of a life connected to others and experiences.

And therein is the gift of clarity that sadly, many times only comes from crisis. Life is so much easier for me with a strong, clear, and authentic set of values to give me a governing motivation and perspective for life.

At forty-nine and becoming a dad, my male bravado disappeared in a flurry of nappies, bows, and pretty dresses. I've never felt so vulnerable and unsure, more scared about the measles, scuffed knees and snot noses with the possibility of not being able to protect against broken bones and hearts!

www.michaelray.com.au

PAUL BEARDMORE

A DAD IN DISTRESS

FINDING HOPE THROUGH MY SONS SMILE

"As he lay there in that hospital bed I realised, that if he can
smile through everything he had been through, that I could too
and that nothing I could go through
could ever be that bad."

I always considered myself a manly man, someone who was tough and could handle whatever was thrown at me. As a young man I worked in mustering camps in the Northern Territory and the Kimberly. I later went on to drive road trains throughout some of the most remote parts of Australia. I didn't think much could worry me, but I soon discovered I was wrong and found myself vulnerable.

On July 6, 2011, my world was turned upside down and I soon discovered how vulnerable I really was. This day began like any other. I was on a day off from work and sitting at home having a coffee after the gym. Out of the blue my ex-wife called me. But because I had not been allowed to speak to my children since Easter that year, I was very hesitant to answer the call. She had made things very difficult for me and my children and had made a number of unfounded allegations.

I eventually answered and when I did, I heard the words, *"Lane has been hurt and is in a rescue helicopter on his way to the Royal Children's Hospital."* She also said, "Oh, by the way, we don't live in Bundaberg anymore we now live in Oakey." She had moved to a dairy farm with her then boyfriend whom I had suspected of being violent. Suspicions that later proved to be correct.

With this news I went into panic mode. I madly tried to book a flight to Brisbane for myself and my partner. To add to the stress, Darren Lockyer was playing his last game ever in a State of Origin, skyrocketing the cost of flights and making availability very difficult.

I rang the hospital from the airport for an update on my son's condition and was told that they couldn't tell me because I wasn't family. They said it was okay, his 'father' was there with him. I informed the lady that I was in fact his father and the man who was there was his mother's boyfriend. It was at this point that she informed me that he was not in a good place and was on life support in an induced coma. It was right there in the packed airport terminal that I lost it and became a blubbering mess.

The flight to Brisbane which normally took an hour and fifteen minutes was the longest flight of my life. It felt as though I could have run quicker. We arrived at the hospital and were told that we would have to sit outside the ward until my ex-wife and her partner left.

I demanded that police and child safety be contacted immediately as I had concerns over the cause of the 'accident'. I had also previously contacted the Department of Child Safety and Queensland Police over concerns for my children's safety. In both cases I felt frustrated as it seemed to my knowledge, that not much more had been done than a knock on the door by the police asking if my kids were okay. I felt my pleas for help went unheard and, in my view, they just regarded me as a disgruntled ex-husband.

Neither the police or child safety ever attended the hospital and in fact over the next few days, I had been repeatedly asked by social workers to sit down and talk to my ex-wife's partner about what had happened to Lane as it would make him feel better. They may have thought they were doing the right thing, but in my opinion, were very misguided. All they were doing was adding to my stress. Lane was under the care of my ex-wife and her then partner (now ex). I did then, and still to this day, hold them responsible for what happened. Having had her partner previously threaten me, he along with his six-foot four frame, came across to me as a very aggressive and intimidating individual. I had been told stories about his past, and whilst not sure if true, I had a sense that he was a violent person. Having a social worker trying to make me hear his bullshit story was not going to make things better for anyone.

The police in fact took three weeks before they even looked at the case. After repeated calls and a drive out to Toowoomba for a face-to-face meeting to seek answers about the lack of investigation, still nothing was forthcoming. One detective asked me what I really hoped to achieve. Without an investigation, they had decided that it had been an accident. Another detective from child protection told me that 'accidents just happen' and I should 'get over it'. This was despite there being several definitive avenues of evidence, including the threats and anonymous phone calls I'd received which had been proven to be the partner. He also had numerous domestic violence orders against him and had been restricted from seeing his own children.

The incident should have been investigated immediately as a four-year-old child had been nearly killed and there was only one witness which is supposed to signal police attending immediately. He had shown his true colours when he became aggressive with my ex-wife and was forcibly removed by police from the parent's lodge at the hospital. A few months later he seriously assaulted her and her brother which resulted in him serving a jail term.

The original diagnosis given for my son was 'he would never talk, would be wheelchair bound and would be tube fed for the rest of his life'. He spent two weeks on life support, five weeks in a coma and five months in hospital. I remember one of the hardest days I have ever had was when the doctors decided to test his brain activity to decide if his life support should be turned off. While doing this the family of the child in the bed next to him were saying goodbye as they were about to turn off his life support.

While doing the test Lane had a fit. I walked over and grabbed his hand and started talking to him and the nurse said to me, "keep talking to him he knows you are there." With that I again started to cry – I was overcome with relief that he was still in there; he just had to wake up.

Through the next five months he went through copious amounts of rehabilitation. It was there that I gained an immense pride and respect not just for his resilience but the attitude he faced every challenge with. He never once complained and faced every challenge with a smile. After five months he walked out past the same neurosurgeon that gave the original diagnosis, high fived him and said, "see you later mate." The staff called him "The Miracle Boy".

Seeing him suffer so much yet watching him never once complain about anything he went through became my lightbulb moment. If he can smile through everything, I can too and nothing I could go through could ever be that bad. He was and still is my hero. He is my happy place and the one that I look up to when I think life sucks. Still to this day he is my 'Why'. Thankfully he had helped me develop this mindset as more was yet to come.

As if going through what we went through with Lane was not traumatic enough, on February 9, 2013, eighteen months after Lane's injury, at 4am in the morning, my partner and I were woken by an aggressive bashing on the door. We answered it to two detectives and three uniformed police officers. "Let us in!" they kept saying, and my partner was asking, "is it one of the kids? What's wrong?" With that we let them in, and they told us to sit down and informed us that there had been an incident down the road. They believed that Shandee, my stepdaughter, had passed away. They wouldn't let us see her and made us make a positive identity by viewing her tattoos.

Over the next eighteen months we sat back and watched as the police tried to solve the case. We had our suspicions on who it was but over time the police mentioned different people whom it could possibly have been. We started thinking it was different people to the one we had originally suspected but we kept coming back to our original suspicions, the ex-boyfriend whom Shandee had been in a very toxic relationship with.

After a protracted investigation the police finally arrested Shandee's ex-boyfriend in September 2014. In March, 2017 the case finally went to trial on completely circumstantial evidence. After a long three-week trial, and given the information that the jury were given, they were left with no alternative but to find him not guilty. We were gutted. We knew that there was a lot more evidence that firmly pointed the finger straight at him but for whatever reason had not been presented to the jury.

It was a very tough period. People we thought were friends, didn't want anything to do with us and other people, some of whom we'd never met and didn't know, decided they wanted to be part of the action. We would feel out of place in public and felt like people were staring at us when we were grocery shopping because we, and more to the point, my wife, had been on the news frequently since the incident. But still there would be no closure. Nor could Shandee's death be put to rest until the coroner's inquest, or so we thought.

The coroner's inquest into her death finally came around in July, 2019. We sat through this for a further three long traumatising weeks having to once again listen to and go through all of the evidence. This time was different though, because this time the accused was made to sit on the stand and answer questions, something that he had never done. This brought up a lot of hurtful memories for us especially as we listened to Shandee's ex-partner tell the court that he had memory problems and that while he could remember every little detail leading up to that night and after that night he couldn't remember where he was or what he did the night she was murdered.

In August 2020, Coroner David O'Connell handed down his findings naming Shandee's ex-boyfriend as the person who was responsible for her death. While this was a great relief that he had been named and the truth had finally come out, it really brought some raw feelings as he had already been found not guilty and there is little chance, he will ever face justice.

Strangely a lot of people comment on how well I have handled everything, but little do they know that I have two faces. I have the 'at home sad face' and then when I walk out into public I put on my smile and that's what people see. Still today, when I am in my struggle place, I look at photos of Lane when he was in hospital and then look at him now singing (he loves to sing) and I instantly go back into my happy place. I have found that you need that one thing that puts that smile back on your face, that brings you back to your happy place and for me that is Lane. His smile is infectious! After seeing his determination and fight to prove doctors wrong and live life to his fullest, He is my hero.

I think that no matter who you are or how tough you are, we all have moments where things seem too hard. To always look at life with a get-back-on-the-horse attitude is the best approach but not always the easiest. It's a must that you find what makes you happy and keep that happy place for when you think life sucks. For me my happy place is my son and remembering how he never gave up. Despite everything stacked against him, he still not only smiled but he made everyone around him smile, and continues to do that today.

Life can be tough, we all have our vulnerable moments. It's how we handle them that matters. Every time we get knocked down we must find that happy place and get back up.

paulbeardmore@bigpond.com

ZAC JONES

CAR CRASH DRIVER AND SURVIVOR
RISING FROM THE ASHES OF ADDICTION

"In my hopelessness, I started a conversation with someone I
hadn't really spoken to in a long time, Myself. As I sat in that
tomb, I made a single promise to myself, 'I'm going to leave jail
in better shape than when I came in'. I learned that no amount of
drugs or alcohol would fix me or my problems. Only I could do
that. I started to believe that I had the ability to rise.
There is a Phoenix in all of us."

My story of hope starts in the most unlikely of places. Prison.

Before I talk about how I found hope in such a hopeless place, I need to take you back to when I was young. I came from a good family. Both my parents worked very hard to provide a good start for me. They each had their faults as all people do, but they really tried their hardest to raise a functioning adult. Our home life, however, was a very toxic environment to grow up in. My parents' marriage fell apart whilst we were living on a small equestrian farm in the Yarra Valley and as a result, I was trapped in the middle of a very ugly marital breakdown. Because of financial reasons my parents were unable to physically separate and so they were forced to live under the same roof for many years.

As time went on the environment became increasingly aggressive, manipulative, and dysfunctional. No-one in our house was coping well, nor were we dealing with our problems in a good way. I became a very angry and frustrated young teenager. When I was at home, I would spend my time looking for anything I could destroy and pour my anger out on. I had no idea at the time why I felt the way I did or how to cope properly with it, so I was desperately looking for any outlet or way to cope with my emotions. I was trapped on a farm and couldn't turn to anyone for help. When I wasn't at home I was at school, and as my parents' marriage continued to spiral out of control, I became less and less interested in learning, or hearing what the teachers had to say. Very soon I began to aim my anger and frustration at the school environment, disrupting classes, damaging school property, picking fights, generally breaking any rules I could.

The more trouble I got in at school the less I cared about the consequences. I would get caught smoking and selling cigarettes, defacing school property or fighting. The school would call my parents to come and pick me up. I would get yelled at and receive a lecture, which I would tune out of, and then at the end I would apologise and do it all again the next day. This became a habit very quickly. It would usually culminate in me being expelled from one school, then being re-enrolled in a different school mid-semester - where the cycle would repeat, again and again.

I was carrying so much emotion around with me and I had no idea how to deal with it. It was like trying to drag myself through each passing day with a semi-truck tied around my waist. I began self-harming when I was about 13. Then one day I was at school and one of the older kids bought some weed to school. I'd never tried it but I really wanted to, so I didn't hesitate to smoke it with him.

Almost immediately I fell in love with how it made me feel. I didn't feel angry, or stressed or spiteful or broken. I didn't really feel anything. My head had gone from a bull pit during a market crash on Wall Street, to a quiet garden sanctuary. It was as if all my problems had melted away. For the first time in my teenage years, I floated carelessly through the day. That night I got home to the usual sound of my parents fighting, but this time it was as if they were trying to yell at each other with mouths full of cotton wool. I was almost deaf to it. In my head I had just found the answer to all my problems.

I woke up the next day sober and the magic had worn off. Everything was back to normal again. From that moment on I had to get high. I had to get back to that place I had been. I actively sought out drugs any chance I could. With great success I managed to meet a few dealers who spent most of their time hanging around train stations. They were really easy to get to on my way to and from school, which after a while I would skip completely to go and get high.

Naturally my parents found out and tried to intervene, but in truth it was too late. I was already addicted, not in the chemically addicted sense of the word, but addicted to the feeling of escaping my problems, escaping reality and being numb. I would try harder and harder to hide it, and my parents would always catch me out eventually. This game of cat and mouse turned in my favour when my parents eventually managed to go their separate ways. My Mum and I moved into a house in the suburbs. The one rule of living under her roof was "no drugs". Which also happened to be the one rule I refused to abide by.

No matter what mum did she could not get through to me, and as it went on, I realised that she couldn't really do anything to stop me. What I also realised was that I wasn't on a farm anymore. There was a bus stop right out the back gate of our house, so I could leave whenever I wanted. Pretty soon I began couch-surfing at random people's houses and hanging out at train stations and shopping centres every day. I woke up with the goal of getting as off my face as possible. Day in and day out I succeeded in achieving just that.

The thing is, when you're constantly under the influence of drugs and alcohol you feel as though nothing bothers you. That you are not receptive to emotional trauma, that you aren't nursing mental health problems. When in actual fact all of these things are bubbling away under the surface. I hadn't dealt with any of my trauma from my parents' marriage breakdown. I was still angry at them and resentful for what I had been forced to deal with. I was angry because I hated school and couldn't fit in, which made me feel like a reject.

There were a million problems that all went unattended to. I had become so dependent on drugs in such a short time, that I had no capacity to process or deal with my emotions in any other way than to continue taking them. Which does not resolve anything. In fact as I have learned, it just allows that grass fire of trauma to grow into a full on bushfire, which time and time again, will manifest itself into violent and self-destructive behaviour. This is observable in anyone battling addiction or substance abuse.

And so trips to the principal's office in school turned into trips in the back of police cars to the station, where my mum would have to come and sit in during police interviews and hear all the horrible things I had been doing. Whether damaging public property, stealing alcohol or stealing cars, she had to sit and watch in absolute despair as I was charged, fingerprinted, photographed, and bailed to appear before a magistrate time and time again. Often, she would not see or hear from me for months, only to get a phone call from the police saying that I was yet again in custody. She would take me home, we would argue, I would refuse to stay off the drugs and I would leave again. This cycle went on for many years as I descended further and further into drug addiction. I was using a cocktail of many different substances and my physical and mental wellbeing all declined.

I battled with drug and alcohol addiction throughout my teenage years and into my early twenties. During this time, I got jumped and had my jaw fractured, crashed my first car, lost my license and had several very toxic and abusive relationships. I'd attempted suicide and had committed a lot of very serious crimes, either for financial gain or as shameful as it is to admit, for the sheer thrill of it.

I had become a wreck. Anyone could be forgiven for thinking I was a lost cause. Too far gone to save.

The question is always asked. "How do you help someone battling with addiction, how do you save someone from going off the rails?"

The answer offers little hope unfortunately. Quite simply you can't. You cannot do anything to help, or reason with someone who is in the pit of an addiction, and you can very well get dragged down by continuing to try and help them. Like the age old saying goes, you can't help someone who won't help themselves.

So, until that person reaches whatever their personal rock-bottom is, and decides they want to change, then there is no help that you can really give them.

There have been several times in my life where I thought I had hit rock-bottom. Or maybe I've just been there several times in my life. But whichever it is, it got to the point where despite my mum's best efforts, she knew there was nothing she could say or do to stop me from going down the road I was so doggedly travelling. So, she cut ties with me. As hard as it must have been for her, she couldn't keep letting herself get hurt. I genuinely believe that was the right thing for her to do.

When I was twenty, I moved into a rental property that my mum and her partner owned with her close friends. It was a chance for me to get a good rental record behind me and it was a nice little place. At the time when I moved in I had just jumped into a new relationship. I hastily moved her in with me which was a massive mistake, because our relationship quickly took a very nasty turn. It became a very volatile environment; made only worse by the amount we were both drinking.

I had surrounded myself with other guys who like me, abused drugs, binge-drank and behaved recklessly. When I got my own place it became a party house very quickly. A place where everyone came to get smashed and behave like animals.

Between working really long hours as a labourer, I was constantly fighting with my abusive girlfriend, using drugs and alcohol daily and then binge-drinking with my mates every other day. Faster than ever, I began spiralling out of control. So quickly in fact, I moved into the rental property on the 11th of November and on the 9th of December, all my years of drug and alcohol abuse and reckless behaviour, culminated in one violent crash.

During an otherwise typical night of binge-drinking, drug taking and stupid behaviour, at about 12am, after sculling the last of our alcohol, vodka straight from the bottle, my mate in-between bouts of projectile vomiting, suggested we go and buy more. On the other side of the city there was an all-night bottle shop that I'm ashamed to say, I had driven drunk to on several occasions.

Without a second thought I reached for my keys and walked to my car. I should note that I had very literally only just finished taking turns with my vomiting friend sculling from a full bottle of vodka. We, without a second thought jumped into my car and were about to pull out of the driveway, when three other friends of ours jumped in as well, because they wanted to come with us.

This car ride was doomed from the start. Proof of that lies in the fact that, as I reversed out of my driveway, I actually backed into a car parked across the street. Right then and there I should have pulled back into the driveway and called it a night. Had I have done that the events that followed would never have happened.

Unfortunately, that is not what I did. When I backed into the car, we all shared an awkward look and then of all things, laughed, as I put my car in drive and continued on our way.

My impaired state deteriorated at an alarming rate. All the vodka I had just sculled began hitting my system all at once. I was swerving from one side of the road to the other, unable to see straight, regulate my speed or even figure out where I was going. After several wrong turns my front passenger pulled up Maps on his phone but was too drunk himself to see the directions. I carelessly looked down at his phone. When I looked back up it was too late, we were heading for a brick wall. And then everything went black.

I came to with my hands still holding the wheel. Where was I? Why was I in my car? I looked around and could not make sense of what I was looking at. I heard panicked voices rushing around the car. I heard confused mumbling from my passengers. Suddenly a fire extinguisher was blasted at the car. I was in total shock, and I sat there disoriented and dazed, until I was freed from the car and put on a stretcher. As I was loaded into an ambulance, I caught a glimpse of what had happened.

Paramedics, police, and firemen rushed around trying to get everyone out of the car. All I could say was 'What have I done?' That's the last thing I remember.

I woke up in hospital completely naked with people rushing around me. I asked where my friends were. Are they okay? No-one had any answers. My mum turned the corner and the second I saw her all I could say was I'm sorry. A nauseous feeling stirred in my stomach. I barely had time to say I was going to be sick before, as if on instinct, my mum yanked a wheelie bin in front of me and I hurled vomit into it. The smell cleared the room. Mum stayed a little while longer but eventually left. And when she did I lay in that cold hospital room alone, with the weight of my guilt, shame and fear pushing down on me. I had a million questions and not a single answer.

In the days, weeks and months following my crash, I slipped further off the edge of the world. I was crushed, defeated, and broken. I felt guilty, ashamed, and hopeless. I hated myself. And so, I treated myself poorly and continued to let myself be treated poorly. As far as I had fallen, even this wasn't my rock-bottom. I had to attend a police station a few weeks after the crash and was charged with numerous counts of negligently causing serious injury and reckless conduct endangering life. But I was bailed to appear before a judge. I met with a lawyer who told me to get my affairs in order because I was going to jail.

The weight of knowing that nothing you do anymore would make a difference, was almost more than I could bare. In my mind it didn't matter if I turned my life around and it didn't matter if I was sorry, I was going to be punished for what I did. Rightfully so. But I wrote myself off completely, abusing drugs and alcohol even worse than before. I even began using needles. I slumped into the darkest pit I've ever known, and there I stayed, wallowing in the abyss of my own creation.

Anyone could be forgiven for thinking I was too far gone to help and that the story of Zac Jones would not have a happy ending. I believed that myself for a long time.

Whilst my perception of time was frozen, in the land of the living time kept on going, and after eighteen months I was put before a judge at the County Court. I watched my friends and mother sob uncontrollably, as the judge and prosecution read out the events that took place the night of my crash and stated that a term of imprisonment was the only fitting punishment.

I battled the entire time trying to keep a poker face on. I fought back tears to try and make the situation easier on my loved ones. Perhaps, I thought, if I don't show how it's affecting me then it might not hurt them as badly.

My attempt at a blank face offered little solace as the judge read out my sentence. Four years nine months, with a non-parole period of two and a half years. In my head I tried to focus on the non-parole period. I attempted to make it sound small in my head, two and a half years. 'Ok that's thirty months'. No that still sounded like a long time. 'Ok nine hundred and twelve days'. No that was worse. Nothing made it any better. And shortly after receiving my sentence I was escorted in cuffs through the back of the courtroom and into a tiny elevator, where it felt as though I was descending into hell.

I was strip-searched and then placed in a holding cell.

As I got dressed again, a chilling thought crept up my spine whilst I looked at the cold and dirty painted concrete walls around me, at the blocked stainless-steel toilet filled with human waste, at the impregnable metal door confining me to this morgue like room.

'My life is over.' At that moment a part of me crumbled. I had nothing; I was nothing. I was a broken junkie left with nothing more than a head full of demons and self-hate.

'Four years nine months.'

The Judges words ricocheted around my head like shrapnel piercing my skull.

Was this going to be my life, my story?

In my hopelessness I started a conversation with someone I hadn't really spoken to in a long time. Myself. I had no control over what happened to me from here on out, I had no way out of this situation but to go through it. The lack of control over my own life was frightening. But at the same time, I also had a moment of extreme clarity - a lightbulb moment. What I realised, was that the only thing I did have control over, was myself. What happened to me next was not up to me, but how I responded was absolutely in my control. This small fact gave me a slither of hope, something to hold on to. I told myself that this time will either make or break me. It will be my uprising or my undoing. And either outcome was totally up to me.

As I sat in that tomb I made a single promise to myself.

'I'm going to leave jail in better shape than when I came in'.

It was a something to focus on, a simple objective to work towards. It could be anything. But I was going to keep that promise at the forefront of my mind.

I was 60kg wringing wet, skin and bone. I was a drug addict. I hated myself. My head was a complete mess, I had f***** up my entire life and now I was completely alone.

Frankly a good sleep and a decent meal would have put me in better shape than I was in. Nevertheless, in that moment I thought to myself,

'What can I do right now, here in this cell, to better myself'?

A voice at the back of the room in my head called out like an impatient heckler at a comedy show.

'F*** it, you might as well do some push-ups!'

The idea made me chuckle. Because I was tired, completely drained emotionally and physically. Withdrawals were already setting in and I was in the clothes I wore to court - a long sleeve white shirt and trousers. But I got down on that floor and started doing push-ups until I failed. Then I'd take a minute rest and do it again. I kept doing push-ups until the guards came to get me to put me on the bus to jail. Their judgmental looks at me sweating on the floor of the cell didn't affect me. I knew what I was doing and I was in control.

Making a promise to yourself is easy. But when the reality of it sets in, you realise just what it's going to take to honour that promise. However, failure was not an option. In my mind it was sink or swim. About a month into my sentence, I was really not doing well, the weight of my circumstances was crushing me. On top of that, I had so much poison festering away in my head. All my guilt, shame, regret, anger and filth was rotting me from the inside out. Infectious waste, the bi-product of the life I had led. I had to purge myself, find a way to get this toxic sludge out of my body. How long had I been like this I wondered - is this what I had been covering up with the drugs and alcohol, what I had been running from all these years?

I wanted to get it all out of me. The only way I could think of to do that was to put it down on paper, but where would I start?

On the phone to my mum one day, despite how far apart we had fallen, somehow, we landed on the same page. Mum mentioned to me that she had thought about writing a book, writing our story. It all clicked in my head. I said I'd been thinking the same thing and after a short phone call we had agreed we would start writing straight away.

This was it, I was going to put everything down on paper, get it all out where I can see it and deal with it. I wrote every day, as much as I could until my hand ached and I couldn't hold a thought. It helped pass the long sleepless nights and would often leave me so drained I would actually get a good night sleep.

The first six months of my sentence were the hardest. Transferred from jail to jail, then unit to unit, then cell to cell. Packing up my few possessions was harder than you think. Just as you get used to your surroundings, you get moved and start again. On top of that I was battling with withdrawals and cravings every day. At night I would dream of using drugs I didn't want to use, but my body and mind did. I would cry and contemplate killing myself often. I would dismantle my shaver and take the razor blades in my hand with the intent on slicing myself from my palm to my elbow, but I'd hurt the people who loved me enough. No easy way out, you have to be the one to suffer through this.

The angry voices in my head would shout and yell over the top of one another at night making it impossible to sleep, and I would have no choice but to listen and yell back. I was fighting every day to regain control of my head. So every day I kept my promise to myself in the forefront of my mind. I kept writing, I kept training at the gym, and I kept going to see the psychologist every week to help work through my problems.

On top of all of my own issues, I was navigating my way through the pressure cooker that was jail. There is no such thing as keeping your head down in jail. You get sucked into the politics and culture one way or another. I had to stand on my own two feet. I had to fight to defend myself and always stay alert. I went from hating being locked in at night to realising it was the only time I could relax and let my guard down. So night times became incredibly productive. I would write our book, write songs and eventually when I got my hands on a guitar, I would practice and play them.

During my time locked in at night, I realised what I wanted and what I didn't. What I loved and what I hated. I learned who I was again, and I killed the parts of myself that were holding me back. Night after night I incinerated everything I used to be until it was ash. And from those ashes rose a new man, a better man. A man that I came to like and respect. A Phoenix.

My time in jail was the hardest thing I've ever had to endure, and my family had to endure it in their own way too. But I truly believe that as a result of the path I took in jail, it saved my life. In the strangest way it was the best thing that ever happened to me. Because I CHOSE to make it that way.

I was released on parole December 6, 2021, just over two and a half years after my sentencing. I walked out the front gate, having kept my promise to myself to leave in better shape than when I came in, towards my crying mum with my arms wide open. As we drove away from the jail with music blaring, the barbed wire and tall fences shrunk into the distance of our rear view mirrors. Leaving behind all of our misery, leaving behind the ashes of who I used to be. Taking with us the strength, lessons and perspective we had both gained. Celebrating our reforged relationship and vowing to share our story of hope and use it to help others. I was free.

Since being released from jail we have published our book called 'Why The Fallen?' It is available on our website www.whythefallen.com and we are slowly getting it into book stores. I now participate in different public speaking engagements with troubled teens and young drivers to prevent them from making the same mistakes as I did. I do interviews with different podcasters and take every opportunity to help others. I work full time and am going to start releasing the music I wrote while I was in prison. I also got a large ink Phoenix tattooed on my chest to symbolise the transformation I underwent, and to always remind me of just how far I have come.

TM

I learned that everything that had happened to me and where I ended up was of my own doing. Facing the consequences gave me an opportunity to grow, to be better and to do well. And I learned that the strength and resilience, the discipline and courage to face any situation was within me. I learned that no amount of drugs or alcohol would fix me or my problems. Only I could do that.

Believe that you have the ability to rise. There is a Phoenix in all of us.

https://whythefallen.com

ACKNOWLEDGEMENTS

I could have never made this book happen on my own. Thank you to the 15 brave men who have written their stories to share on the pages of this book. They have allowed themselves to be vulnerable, real and raw with one goal in mind, to let other men know '*it's okay to talk about how you really feel and on the other side of this, hope can be found*'.

They share their journeys of regret, shame, heartache, disappointment, and resilience but more importantly that *Pivotal moment of HOPE* that led them to *wake up* and realise that change could be made on the other side. The stories of all these men and every man and women who have shared their stories with me for Stories of HOPE Australia and Worldwide over the past five years have truly changed my life. I thank you and am so grateful for every single one of you.

A special thank you to the Sands Tavern in Maroochydore QLD who gave us our humble beginning. It was a space to call home each month allowing us to reach out and impact our local community. The place where stories were shared by everyday people and Stories of HOPE vol 1 and 2 found their inspiration before Covid morphed us into an online community. The stories of the 15 men in this book have come out of those difficult two years where the spirits of many were crushed and my desire grew to bring hope to many around the world as I connected up with and interviewed many men to share their stories of resilience over adversity empowering others to never give up in the process.

To my husband, Marty, who probably never realised when he married me the extent to which he would have to share me with the rest of the world. Thank you for allowing me the freedom to be myself and for encouraging my passion for helping the lost, broken, downtrodden, and lonely to find happiness. Together we are a great team, working towards helping others find HOPE in an ever-changing world.

To my son, Josh, thank you for all your help in creating this book and for your endless hours of advice helping me to create and make decisions on the cover of this book along with the endorsements and other content to make it appealing to men. It has been invaluable having your advice and ideas as someone who works in a very male dominated industry and understands well the complexities of men and what they face. You are not only a wonderful son and husband yourself, but a very caring and compassionate person who has been a great mate and a shoulder to lean on for many men of all ages who have struggled in life. You have such a positive nature the rare ability to make everyone smile when they are around you, no matter how bad they are feeling. You have always encouraged me and made me believe that anything is possible. I am so grateful and blessed that you are my son.

To my beautiful daughter, Aleisha, the girl in my life who has truly shown me unconditional love. You are a great reprieve from the intensity of life with your fabulous sense of humour which cracks me up when I need it the most. You are wise beyond your years and bring me so much joy and laughter. You are such a blessing. Thank you for being someone who is an amazing listener and who gives me time to talk things out when I just need a sounding board. I am so proud of the resilient and amazing person you are. You are the most incredible daughter and friend anyone could ever wish for.

To my son-in-law, Joel, granddaughters, Aali and Mia, and daughter-in-law, Kalina, I love you more than words can say. You enrich our family so much.

Thank you to my mum and dad, who are no longer in this world. They taught me what it is to truly love others unconditionally. To my brothers, Carl and Russel, thank you for always being there for me. Thank you for being such important and supportive caring men in my life. We will always be the 3 three Fishers.

To my extended family and all my friends out there—and there are so many—who have helped me on my journey to form and carry out my vision. Friendship means so much to me and I value each and every one of you and your contribution to my life. Thank you. It is because of you all that I am sharpened.

Thank you to all who have assisted me in the process of writing this book and a big thankyou to my gifted and talented publisher Jennifer Sharp for helping make this happen. Thank you to Matt Druce, Monique Parker and Bec Cheney who have encouraged me and supported me with my marketing of Stories of HOPE and to Alex Gerrick and the team at 'FearLess' for all your support over the past three years and for choosing me as an ambassador for your wonderful PTSD organisation which has given me a vehicle to spread Stories of HOPE even further.

Thank you to the following men who I have great admiration for who have written endorsements for my book: my long term Stories of HOPE team member Ex Detective Stuart Rawlins, Mental health advocate and former NRL player Darius Boyd, Former BBC journalist and founder of Baton Of Hope Mike McCarthy and Journalist Jason Dasey who wrote the forward for this book.

To all my Stories of HOPE community thank you for your ongoing support. To my team of speakers, and all those individuals around the world who have shared their stories with me who have caught a glimpse of my vision and bared their souls in order to change lives and show everyone out there who are going through hard times. You are an inspiration and show that life and great purpose after hard times is definitely possible.

Knowing you all and what you have been through continues to encourage and inspire me on a daily basis to keep running with and expanding my vision to reach as many people out there in the far corners of the earth with this message: Together is better and there is always HOPE.

If you have been touched by this book and would like to have Kerrie or one of the contributors speak at your event, please visit our website:

www.storiesofhope.com.au
info@storiesofhope.com.au

You can purchase more books in this series - Volume One: Stories of HOPE Everyday People, Extraordinary Stories and Volume Two: Stories of HOPE Resilient People, Remarkable Stories from www.storiesofhope.com.au

Stay tuned as more books in the Stories of HOPE series are released.

Read more inspiring stories from remarkable men and women and know that whatever you are going through, you are not alone and - there is always HOPE.

www.ingramcontent.com/pod-product-compliance
Lightning Source LLC
Chambersburg PA
CBHW070019120726
47909CB00003B/1000